THE ITALIAN'S
FUTURE BRIDE

THE ITALIAN'S FUTURE BRIDE

BY

MICHELLE REID

MILLS & BOON®

First published in Great Britain 2006
Large Print edition 2007
Harlequin Mills & Boon Limited,
Eton House, 18-24 Paradise Road,
Richmond, Surrey TW9 1SR

© Michelle Reid 2006

ISBN-13: 978 0 263 19447 0
ISBN-10:   0 263 19447 7

Set in Times Roman 16¼ on 26 pt.
16-0507-57157

Printed and bound in Great Britain
by Antony Rowe Ltd, Chippenham, Wiltshire

CHAPTER ONE

IT WAS like playing Russian roulette with your sex life: place a loaded invitation in the barrel, then shoot and see if you scored a hit.

Everyone was doing it, Raffaelle Villani observed cynically—the young and nubile, complete with breast implants and carefully straightened and dyed blonde hair. They circled the room eyeing up likely victims, picked the richest man they could find, then primed him and fired their lucky shot.

Or unlucky, depending from which side of the fence you viewed it.

Some you win, some you lose, he mused as one eager player tried the deal on him only to be rewarded with the sight of his back.

Contempt twisting his lean golden features, he beat a retreat to the furthest corner of the room where the bar was situated. Discarding his un-touched glass of champagne, he ordered a glass of full-blooded red wine to take its place.

Functions like this were the pits and he would not have come but for his stepsister twisting his arm. He owed Daniella a favour for pulling him out of a tricky situation recently with a woman who had been about to become his latest lover—until Daniella had whispered in his ear that the woman was married with a small son.

It turned out that she had even lied to him about her name. Discovering that she was actually the ex-catwalk model Elise Castle, now married to the heavyweight Greek Leo Savakis, had not made Raffaelle feel good about himself.

Married women were not his bag. Married women with small children were an even bigger turn-off. As were neat little liars who pretended to be someone they were not. Elise Castle ticked the boxes in all three categories and the hardest part of it all had been accepting how thoroughly he had been duped by a pair of innocent blue eyes and a set of good breasts that had been her own.

Or maybe not, Raffaelle then contended. Perhaps the breasts and the blue eyes had been just more lies the beautiful Elise had fed to him. Fortunately he had not managed to get close enough to find out.

But he still owed it to Daniella that he'd

managed to get out of a potentially scandal-spinning tangle before it had exploded in his face.

He was into gun metaphors, he noticed. What a great way to spend a Saturday night.

Where was Daniella—?

Straightening his six-foot-four-inch frame up from its bored languid slouch against the bar, Raffaelle began scanning the sea of bodies milling about in front of him for a glimpse of the sylphlike figure belonging to his beautiful stepsister.

He found her almost instantly. Her glossy mane of black hair and the red dress she was wearing made her virtually impossible to miss. She was standing with some smooth-looking guy over by a wall on the other side of the room, and it came as a shock to Raffaelle to see that she was playing the game like all the rest!

She was pouting, her pose distinctly saucy, her breasts pushed up almost against the guy's chest while he looked down at her with one of those lazy I'm-interested-smiles on his handsome face.

Were Daniella's breasts her own—?

The question hit Raffaelle's brain and made him curse softly because he didn't care what Daniella's breasts were made of. She was not and never had been his type. And anyway, as his step-sister, she was and always had been off limits.

She was also getting married in two months, to one of his closest friends. But there she stood, coming on to another man!

Annoyance launched him away from the bar with the grim intention of going over there and hauling her away before one of the other kind of circling vultures here—the press—noticed her and ruined the foolish creature's life.

'Mr Villani?' a husky female voice spoke to him. 'I'm really sorry to bother you but...'

Raffaelle spun on his heel to find himself staring down at yet another nubile young thing with the requisite blonde hair and good breasts. His expression turned to ice as he looked down at her, though the way she was looking up at him through tense, apprehensive, big blue eyes almost made him think twice about turning his back.

More so when the pink tip of her tongue arrived to nervously calm the little tremor he could see happening with her lips.

Nice lips, he noticed. Full, very pink, very lush lips.

'Do you think I could h-have a word with you?' she requested nervously. 'It's really important,' she added quickly. 'I need to ask you a big favour…'

A favour? Well, that was a novel approach. Raffaelle felt the corner of his mouth give a twitch—and thereby did the worst thing he could have done, by allowing a chink of interest to stop him from walking away.

Her silky hair hung dead straight to her slender shoulders and she possessed the most amazing pearly-white skin. He sent his eyes skimming down her front to her cleavage where two firm, plump very white breasts balanced precariously inside the tiny bodice of the short and skimpy pale turquoise silk thing he supposed he should call a dress. She wasn't tall by his standards, but she had a pair of legs on her that did not need the four inch heels she was wearing to extend their fabulous length.

Cosmetically enhanced or not, this one was probably the most appealing package in the room tonight, he accepted as he lifted his eyes back to the pair of pink lips to watch them tremble some more as she waited for his response.

When he still did not give one, she took a step closer, her too-blue eyes lighting up with appeal. 'You see I have this—problem…'

She was going to touch him. His stupid hesitation had given her encouragement to believe that he was interested.

Raffaelle stiffened, each well toned muscle in his long lean framework abruptly tightening up.

'No,' he iced out.

Then turned on his heel and strode off.

Cold, rude, arrogant swine, Rachel mentally tossed after him in stinging frustration. Did the too-tall, dark and disgustingly handsome devil think he was so special that he didn't need to be polite to a woman?

Well, you're not my type, Mr Villani, she told the long length of his retreating figure. Especially if *his* type was the kind of women doing the rounds here tonight.

Rachel's blue eyes turned bitter as she flicked them round the gathered assembly of the famously rich and beautiful—in that order, money being the biggest attraction here tonight. It was a trade fair for the beautiful people to ply their wares in front of London's wealthiest, though it hid under the more respectable title of a Charity Fundraising Event.

She should not have come here. If Elise hadn't convinced her it was the only way to get close to a man like Raffaelle Villani, she would not have been seen dead at a do like this.

'He likes them blonde and slinky,' Elise had said. 'Notoriously can't keep his hands off. You only have to read down the list of his last fifteen girl-friends to know the man has no control when he's faced with blonde hair and a great pair of legs.'

Well, not in my case, Rachel thought heavily as she gave a grim tug at the hem of the dress Elise had made her wear. 'You have to look the part,' her half-sister had insisted. 'When you pay the extortionate price for tickets like these it means you have to look as if you can afford to throw good money away.'

The silly price of the tickets was one thing, but a five figure sum dress only earned its price tag if it looked good on the wearer.

Rachel felt as if she looked like a very cheap tart.

'Hello, beautiful…' The unremarkable hit line arrived as a hand squeezed around her waist at the same time and a pair of lips arrived at one of the straps which held up the dress. 'Having trouble with the dress? Can I help?'

His teeth nipped at the shoulder strap. Rachel heaved in a thick breath of disgust. 'Take your hands and your teeth off me,' she iced out, then broke free and walked off without giving the guy a single glance.

She'd taken about five steps before she realised she'd inadvertently walked in the same direction as Raffaelle Villani.

And there he was.

She stopped dead.

He was in the process of disentangling a lovely young thing wearing red from the possessive clutches of another man. The vision in red turned to pout a protest at him, then flung her arms around his neck and kissed him full on the mouth.

So much for him preferring them blonde, Rachel thought cynically. The creature he'd just claimed and was now kissing was hot-lipped, glossy and black-haired.

Oh, God, she thought helplessly, what was she going to do if she did not manage to pull this off?

'You're drunk,' Raffaelle informed Daniella.

'Tiddly,' his half-English stepsister insisted with a smile gauged to melt his irritation away.

It did not succeed. 'Admit to being drunk, *cara*,' he advised as he grabbed both of her hands and dragged them down from around his neck. 'It is the only excuse Gino will accept for what you have just been doing.'

'I haven't been doing anything—!' Eyes the colour of warm dark chocolate opened wide and tried their best to look innocent.

'You were hitting on that guy,' Raffaelle accused her.

'We were flirting, that's all! And what do you think you're doing, Raffaelle?' she protested when he took hold of her hand and turned towards the exit.

'Taking you home,' he clipped out. 'I don't know why I let you talk me into bringing you here in the first place.'

'For some fun?' Daniella offered up.

'I don't do this kind of fun.'

'That's your big problem, Raffaelle,' she informed him as he trailed her behind him. 'You don't *do* anything these days other than work yourself into the ground.'

'My choice.'

'To be a grouch.'

A nerve ticked at the corner of his mouth because she was right: he was becoming grouch—a bitter and cynical grouch.

'All because one woman managed to con you into believing she was pure sweetness and light…'

'As you try to do, you mean?'

'I *am* all sweetness and light!' Daniella insisted.

'And that wasn't very nice,' she complained. 'Nor do I lie or cheat.'

'Tell that to Gino not to me,' Raffaelle countered. 'If he had seen the way you were preparing to wrap yourself around that guy, he would call the wedding off.'

'But Gino isn't here because he prefers to be halfway across the world playing the hot shot tycoon.'

'However, the press *is* here—'

Raffaelle stopped walking as a sudden thought hit him. He swung round to pierce her with a hard stare.

'Is that what this is about?' he demanded. 'Did you drag me out to this thing—which is nothing more than an overpriced knocking shop,' he said with contempt, 'so that you would be caught on camera playing the vamp with some other guy just to punish Gino, knowing that *I* would be on hand to haul you out of trouble before you got yourself in too deep?'

'I hate him,' Daniella announced. 'I might even decide not to marry him. I'm supposed to be the love of his life yet I haven't set eyes on him in two wh-whole weeks!'

The small break in her voice did it. Raffaelle

heard the fight with tears and released a sigh. 'Come here, you idiot.' He pulled her into his arms. 'You know Gino worships the ground you walk upon but he is busy trying to free himself up for that long glorious honeymoon he has planned for you both.'

'He even sounds like he would rather be doing something else when he rings me,' she sniffed into his shirt front. 'I'm not a doormat. I refuse to let him wipe his feet on me!'

Raffaelle shifted his stance.

'You're laughing at me!' Daniella choked out.

'No, I am not.'

What he was actually doing was staring over Daniella's glossy dark head into the cynical blue eyes of the blonde who had approached him a few minutes ago. She was now standing about ten feet away being buffeted by the milling crowd but not noticing because she was too busy looking at him as if he was a snake.

A sting injected itself down the front of his body. The confusing signals she was giving off dressed— or *un*dressed—like she was, while glaring at him like that, were setting his senses on edge.

Who the hell was she, anyway? Why had he not hung around long enough to find out?

Did he want to know?

His eyes cooled and hardened. No, he didn't, he answered his own question. Expensive tarts in expensive dresses were ten-a-Euro to buy in this room. He did not need to buy his women. And this one was more the type for the guy who was approaching her from behind right now and eyeing her up and down as if she was his next tasty snack.

And tasty said it, he found himself reluctantly admitting as he ran a glance down her front until he reached the place where those two fabulous legs came together.

Was the hair at her crotch the same pale gold colour as the hair on her head?

He shifted again, was vaguely aware of Daniella talking into his shirt but didn't hear what she said. That damn inconvenient thing called sexual curiosity was trying to take him over, heating him up like a pot coming to the boil.

The blonde stiffened, tugging his gaze back to her face to clash with the shocked look in her eyes. He realised then that she knew what he had been thinking, her pearly-white skin suffused with heat.

Feeling the spark too, *cara*? his glinting eyes

mocked her. Well hard damn luck because I am not buying.

The approaching man had reached her—a tall fair haired good-looking guy who stepped right in behind her and ran his fingers up her bare arms to her shoulders, then bent to murmur something in her ear.

She quivered—Raffaelle saw it happen. As she slowly blinked her eyes and turned her head sideways so she was no longer looking at him, he watched her sumptuous pink mouth tilt into a smile.

She turns on for any man, he observed grimly.

'Hi,' Rachel said, still stinging at the way Raffaelle Villani had just looked at her as if she was a sex object put on show to be bought.

'Hi to you too,' Mark returned. 'No luck with the appeal approach?'

'Look at him,' she sighed, glancing back at Mr Villani who was now in the process of curving the clinging dark-haired woman beneath the crook of his arm.

What was he, six-three—six four? Rachel found herself giving him a thorough once-over. He had a great pair of shoulders inside the black dinner suit he was wearing, and a mean pair of long powerful legs. His bright white dress shirt gave the honey-gold tones of his skin at his throat a warm, tight, healthy glow that annoyingly made the tip of her tongue grow moist.

He was supposed to be a fantastic athlete, so Elise had said. Watching him as he began guiding the dark-haired woman through the doors which led to the hotel foyer, Rachel could see why. He moved with loose-limbed grace, languid and supple but firm. If you stripped him down to a pair of running shorts she would be prepared to bet you wouldn't see a single ripple of unwanted flesh.

Marital status: single. Age: thirty three. Loves snow-skiing and water-skiing. Owns his own sexy powerboat which he races at the weekend when he has the time. Owns homes in London, Paris, Monaco and, of course, his native Milan. Plus a huge private skiing lodge inside the very prestigious Gigante Park, where he likes to his spend part of his winters refining his no doubt amazing skills on the ski slopes. Inherited his wealth from his heavyweight banking family, then went on to triple that fortune with shrewd investments which pushed him and the Villani name right to the top of the rich list.

He was, in other words, a tall, dark, very good

looking, very *rich* Italian male with a sinful amount of sex appeal and all the conceit and arrogance that came with such an impressive pedigree.

It was no wonder he'd cut her out without giving her a chance to explain herself. A man like him was just too darn precious about his own status as the most eligible catch on the block to think of questioning if a woman might want to approach him for any reason other than to latch on to his great body and his lovely money.

Well, Mr Villani, Rachel told his elegant back. Self-obsessed millionaires are ten-a-penny these days. You only have to look around this room to see that.

But men of honour were a very rare breed indeed.

'I thought Elise said he was only into blondes,' she said to Mark. 'But you can't put a hair between him and that black-haired female, so what chance did I have of getting in there?'

'You idiot,' Mark said. 'Don't you know who the brunette is? That's his flighty stepsister, Daniella Leeson of Leeson Hotels fame. She's about to marry his best friend and that other hotel heavy, Gino Rossi—Don't you ever read any of the stuff I print?'

Rachel gave a slow shake of her head, still

watching Raffaelle Villani as he paused in the foyer, framed like a masterpiece between the two open doors. He was helping his stepsister on with her coat now—all care and attention.

Gorgeous face in profile, honesty forced her to admit. With fantastic high cheekbones and black eyelashes so luxurious she could see even from this far away, how they hovered like sexy dark shadows just above those golden cheeks.

When he'd done with the coat he turned his stepsister round and lifted her chin with a gentle finger, then smiled as he murmured something to make her smile back at him.

So he possessed killer charm too, when he wanted to unleash it, Rachel saw, and did not like the stinging flutter she felt suddenly attack the lining of her lower stomach.

Was this the side of him he'd used on Elise to make the silly fool risk her marriage for him? The way Elise told it, he had done all the chasing while she'd tried to keep him at arm's length.

No chance, Rachel denounced. There was no way any woman could hold this man at arm's length if he did not want to be held there. It was no wonder that poor Elise had dropped like a shot duck into his hands.

'I've ruined everything,' she murmured dully. 'Look, they're leaving.'

'The hell you have,' Mark said brusquely. 'We can't let Elise down after all of this planning. I can still rescue this.'

Grabbing one of her hands, he began pulling her towards the foyer.

'The trouble with you, Rachel, is you insisted on trying the wrong tack on him then blew it. This time you do it the way we planned it, okay? So listen,' instructed the man who got his highs hunting down and catching the rich and famous at their worst. 'I'm going to grab the lovely Daniella's attention. All you have to do is to move in on him the moment I move in on her. I can give you ten seconds at most, so don't hang around and, for God's sake, don't let yourself think! This will be our last chance.'

Their last chance...

They'd reached the foyer by now and Mark's instructions were playing across her tense chest muscles like sharp hammering throbs. Raffaelle Villani and his stepsister were already turning towards the main exit doors.

'Hey—Miss Leeson!' Mark called out. 'Where's your future husband tonight?'

Daniella Leeson paused, then turned on the delicate heels of her shoes, saw Mark with a camera already up at his face and switched on a false smile.

'He's…'

'Get going,' Mark muttered sideways at Rachel.

As if in a dream Rachel let Mark's urgency take her over. Her legs felt like jelly as she moved in. Raffaelle Villani was only just turning to watch his stepsister pose for the hated paparazzi so he didn't see Rachel coming at him from one side. Stepping right in front of him and without daring to think, she threw her arms up and clasped his face between her fingers, then stretched up on tiptoe and crushed her mouth against his.

She didn't know which of them was the more shocked as heat hit her body like mega-watt high voltage. His grunt of surprise vibrated against her lips. Lights flashed, her skin burned, her finger-tips tingled where they pressed against his warm satin tight skin.

Seconds. It took too many seconds for his brain to relay to Raffaelle what was happening and by then her mouth was fusing hot against his. His hands leapt up—it was automatic to close them around a small waist with the intention of pushing her away.

A camera flashed.

He pulled his mouth free, found himself staring down at the same blonde who'd approached earlier. *'Madre de Dio.* What do you think you are doing?' he raked out.

The flash hit him again. She was staring up at him, all big blue apologetic eyes and smudged pink lipstick and her fingers had shifted from his face to the back of his neck.

'Sorry,' she whispered breathlessly. 'But you left me with no other choice.'

She began to pull away. The camera was still flashing. Instead of aiding her withdrawal, Raffaelle tightened his grip on her waist and made her stay exactly where she was.

He was blindingly, blisteringly furious. 'No choice about what?' he bit down at her.

She wriggled against him in an effort to free herself. What happened next made her breath catch and he knew why it did. She was plastered against him like a second layer of skin and the extra physical pressure had brought their lower bodies into contact.

'Dio,' he cursed again.

'Oh, God,' Rachel echoed. 'Y-you—you're…'

'I don't need you to tell me what I already know!' he raked out. 'I just need an explanation as to what the hell you think you are trying to pull off with this!'

'I…'

'Okay kiddo, let's go.'

Let's go…Raffaelle lifted his eyes to the photographer, wondered why he hadn't noticed the camera dangling round his neck before. Then answered his own question with a twist of his mouth. He had been too busy looking at her to notice him in any detail.

'Some set-up,' he gritted.

'Please let me go now.' She tugged at his iron grip on her waist.

'Not even if you decide to faint,' he incised, sparks flying from his eyes as he watched Daniella turn towards them and her eyes give a startled blink.

Indeed, he agreed with her surprised expression. The photographer was already shooting out of the door.

'You,' he raked at his attacker, 'are coming with me to explain yourself.'

Without giving her a chance to protest, he

reached up to yank her claws out of his neck, then let go of one hand and used the other to begin hauling her towards the exit.

'Raffaelle—!' A bewildered Daniella called his name as she hurried after them.

Outside a cool breeze hit his angry face.

Just angry—? He was bloody blindingly livid. His instincts must be dulling for him to get caught out like this.

'Please…' the blonde pleaded.

'Be silent,' he snapped out and his hand tightened its grip on her wrist. He felt her wince; he didn't care. Dino, his chauffeur, drew his limo up at the kerb and climbed out of the car.

Raffaelle strode towards it with his captive almost tripping up behind him on her flimsy sparkling spindle-heeled shoes. 'Grab a cab and take Miss Leeson home,' he instructed his driver.

'But—Raffaelle—?' his stepsister wailed in protest.

He ignored her. He ignored everyone, including the blonde who was still desperately trying to get free. Opening the front passenger door to the limo, he tried to propel her inside.

She dug her heels in. 'I'm not—'

He picked her up and bodily put her into the car.

When she tried to get out again, her mouth opening wide with the intention of screaming for help, he bent swiftly and smothered the sound with his mouth.

He didn't take pleasure from hard angry kisses, he told himself, particularly when he'd just been hit on by a woman who deserved a slap not a kiss. However the kiss gave him a hell of a lot more satisfaction, especially when her muffled scream rolled around his mouth and sent his tongue chasing it.

She quivered. She tasted of champagne and pink lipstick.

By the time he yanked his mouth away again she'd sunk into trembling shock.

'Now, listen to me,' he incised as he locked the seat belt around her. 'I don't know how much your partner in crime was paying you to pull off that stunt, but in case you did not notice, he was not the only sleaze-gathering scum working the room back there. The pack has scented a story and is about to descend on us.'

On that hard warning he straightened, slammed the car door shut, then strode round to the other side while Rachel twisted her head to stare dazedly at the press pack gathering at the main hotel doors. By the time she'd absorbed all of that, Raffaelle Villani had folded himself into the driver's seat next to her—a lean, dark, hard-muscled male with aggression bouncing off him.

His chauffeur had left the engine running. He snaked out a hand and threw the car into drive. They took off with a jerk just as the press pack tumbled over each other with their cameras flashing. Rachel watched as the whole debacle played out like a comic strip. Even his stepsister had her part to play. She was standing by the kerb staring after them while the chauffeur was politely trying to urge her into the back of a black cab.

Mark was nowhere.

Thanks, Mark, Rachel thought helplessly, visualising her darling half-brother rushing off to file his scoop without giving a second thought to what he had left her to face!

Rachel flicked a scared glance at the man sitting beside her, then shivered. If murder had a look to it then he was wearing it.

'Please stop the car so I can get out,' she begged and didn't even care that she was begging.

He didn't answer. Lips clamped together, he sent the car shooting out into the main stream of traffic. Several car horns blared in protest at his pushy arrogance. He ignored those too.

'Look, I know you're angry,' she allowed shakily. 'And I know that you have every right to be, but—'

'*Grazie.*'

'This is kidnap!'

'So sue me,' he gritted. 'That could be fun.'

Fun—? Rachel trembled and shivered as she sat tensely beside him. None of this had been *fun* from the moment she'd allowed Elise and Mark to talk her into it. One minute she'd been perfectly content, hiding away in Devon nursing her broken heart, the next minute she'd found herself staying up here in London with her half-sister and being embroiled in her complicated love-life!

'It w-wasn't what you think—'

'You don't know what I'm thinking.'

'I am *not* being paid to—'

'Hit on me?' he offered when those very same words dried in her throat. 'It is a relief to know I still have some natural pulling power then.'

He had loads of natural pulling power. That was his problem.

'Are you always this obnoxious when you've been caught off your guard?' she flared up on the back of pure agitation. 'So I hit on you—what's new there to a man like you? From what I hear, half the women in Europe have done it at some point in your blessed life—and not all of them because of your sex appeal!'

He sent her a glinting look. 'Did I hear a hint of scorn in your tone then?'

'Yes!' she flicked out. 'Men like you stroll through life as if you own it. You do what you want when you want to do it. You pick your women on looks alone and don't give a care whether they have feelings you could actually wound!'

Something sharp hit his voice. 'I wounded—you?'

'You mean you don't know?' The sarcasm was out before she could stop it.

They'd stopped at a set of traffic lights and he turned in his seat. Instantly the sheer size and power of the man flooded over Rachel like a simmering hot shower. She could feel his eyes skimming her face and her body as he checked her out while flipping through his huge data bank of women, trying to pinpoint who she was. Any second now and he was going to make a connection he could have made hours ago if he'd been more observant.

Rachel felt the stinging temptation to lie, if only to really confuse him, but— 'No,' she said finally.

Someone just like you did that to me, she added inside her head. Then she flicked him a hard resentful glance, heaved in a breath and saved him the bother of further taxing his no doubt phenomenal brain power.

'Elise Castle,' she breathed out.

CHAPTER TWO

THE name had its desired effect, Rachel noticed bitterly, as a long thick silence stretched between them and he didn't say or do a single thing.

She held her breath again while she waited for him to recover and begin spitting out a barrage of angry questions—but still nothing came.

In the end she took the initiative and broke the silence. 'The name means nothing to you?' she gibed.

Other vehicle headlights swished past the car windows, lighting their faces momentarily. Illuminated, she saw only the cold steel of his eyes as they fixed hers like lashing daggers and he kept his silence. In the darkness her gaze dropped for some reason to the single line straightness of his mouth.

A mouth that already felt disconcertingly familiar. She could still taste it. Her tongue even made a passing swipe at her lips in response to the thought.

Headlights lit up the car's interior again, dragging her attention back to his eyes. They'd narrowed and were watching her like a hawk waiting to pin its next victim. Rachel's breathing fell into small jerky fits. Her heart was pounding. He was frighteningly exciting to look at, all well cared for male with just the right balance between sensational good looks and raw masculinity.

Her mouth had to part to aid her quick breathing. He dropped his gaze and the result was a tingling quiver across her lips that sent the tip of her tongue nervously chasing it. Sexual awareness was suddenly alive and cluttering the atmosphere. Rachel felt her breasts grow heavy, their tips pushing out with a terrible knowing sting. He flicked those eyes back to hers again and he knew—he *knew*!

Then the traffic lights decided to change, demanding that he set them moving. She watched as if mesmerised as his dark head shifted back into profile, watched his long-fingered hands as he flipped the car into a slick right turn. More seconds ticked by and her chest felt as if it was burning beneath the pressure she was placing on it by barely breathing at all now.

'The name means plenty to me,' he finally answered. 'And you are not Elise.'

No, Rachel knew she wasn't Elise. She was her younger, less pretty, more sensible half-sister.

More sensible—when? She then scoffed at that. Sensible women did not get themselves into situations like this. Sensible women steered clear of the complicated love lives of others—and especially of frighteningly sexy men like him!

Sensible women did not fall in love with handsome Italians with a rich repertoire of words of love and a killer seduction technique—yet she had done it.

She had to close her eyes as an image of Alonso suddenly appeared in front of her. Tall, dark, beautiful Alonso, who had been so warm and attentive and flatteringly possessive when they had been out together, and so excitingly intense and passionate when naked with her in bed. They'd spent six glorious weeks living together in his apartment overlooking Naples. He'd vowed he loved her. 'I love you—*ti'amo mia bella cara…*' he'd murmured to her in his rich, dark, accented voice and she'd known without a doubt that she loved him.

Rachel shivered.

It was only when the time had come for her to return to England and he'd said, 'We had a wonderful time, hmm, *amore*? It is a shame it now has to end,' that she'd understood what a stupid, gullible, naïve fool she had been.

'I said you are not Elise,' this other Italian with the rich, dark accent prompted.

Rachel opened her eyes and let the real world back in. 'No,' she agreed. 'But very few people will be able to tell that from behind…'

A bell of understanding suddenly clanged loud in Raffaelle's head. Next to come was an action replay of the way this woman had thrown herself on him, followed by several camera flashes. Like a wild beast sniffing danger in the atmosphere, he picked up the scent of a deliberately constructed scandal involving him and the very married Elise.

But it was a scandal he believed he had already diverted. As far as he was aware, the lovely Elise had seen the error of her ways after his last spiked conversation with her on the telephone before he'd broken all contact with her and made his quick exit from London back to Milan. The grapevine, via Daniella, said she had not been seen on the social circuit since.

So what was *this* devious creature up to? Why

had she gone to so much trouble to make out for the camera that she was Elise?

'Explain,' he commanded.

Not this side of midnight, Rachel thought tensely and clamped her lips together. Having come this far, she was not about to scupper everything by getting Mark's story pulled before going to print.

She'd already revealed more than she should have done.

'Look…' she heaved out instead. 'You're not an idiot, Mr Villani. You must know you're asking for trouble taking me against my will like this—so just stop the car and let me out now.'

'Not a chance in hell,' he refused.

And the way he turned his head to slide his eyes up her legs had Rachel tugging jerkily at the short skirt of her dress. She knew that look. It was as old as the human race. She'd let him see her attraction to him; now he was looking over the goods on offer.

'If you honestly think—!'

'Changing your mind about the hit, *cara*?' he taunted. 'Wondering if you might have bitten off more than you can chew with me? Well, let me confirm that you have done.' His voice hardened.

'You made the hit. I bought it. Now you are going to play it my way.'

'You're crazy,' she whispered.

Maybe he was, Raffaelle conceded. But no woman—*no woman*—played games with him and got away with it!

'I'm getting out of this car—' Rachel reached for the door handle. The automatic lock gave a clunk as it fell into place at the same time that he increased their speed.

True—true unfettered fear began to scream in her head as it finally began to sink in what a stupid, crazy, dangerous situation she had managed to get herself into here. What did she know about Raffaelle Villani, other than the details fed to her by Mark and Elise? How did she know he wasn't some kind of mega-rich sex maniac prowling Europe unhindered because his money could buy his victims' silence.

Just as he said, he had bought her…

Her skin began to creep, her fingers closing tightly around her small clutch bag so they felt the reassurance of her cellphone.

How much time did she need to call the police before he reacted?

She dared a quick glance at him, heart hammering, fingers tensely toying with the clasp on her bag. He didn't look like a lunatic, just a very angry man—which he had every right to be, she was forced to admit.

'Your partner in crime did not hang around to protect you,' he taunted grimly next.

He had to mean Mark. 'You don't—'

'Unless he is in one of the cars following behind us, that is…'

Cars—? Rachel twisted around to peer through the rear window.

'There are three back there I can pick out as belonging to the paparazzi,' she was told. 'And there are most likely more of them following not far behind them.'

Twisting forward again, she stared at him. 'But why should they want to follow us?'

'You are not that naïve,' he derided the question, flicking his eyes from the rear-view mirror and back to the road ahead. 'Or you would not have chosen Raffaelle Villani to pull your life-wrecking stunt.'

Life wrecking—? 'N-no.' Rachel gave an urgent shake of her head. 'You don't understand. This was not—'

'Not that it matters,' he interrupted. 'We are here now.'

As in *where*—? Even as Rachel thought the question, one of those shiny new apartment blocks that flanked the river loomed up close. With a spin of the wheel he sent the car sweeping on to its forecourt. He stopped it hard on its brakes and was already out of the car and striding around it to open her door.

Rachel didn't move. She was trembling like mad and her heart was thundering. She didn't look at him either, but just stared starkly ahead.

'Do you get out yourself or do I have to lift you?' he demanded.

Since she'd already learnt the hard way that he was perfectly willing to do the latter, swallowing tensely, Rachel took the more dignified choice, unfastened her seat belt and slid out of the car.

It was an odd sensation to find herself standing close to him. Nor did that sensation make any sense because she'd stood this close once already tonight and thrown herself right against him a second time, yet he hadn't felt this tall or as powerfully built or as dangerous as he did right now.

She shivered, panicked and was about to make a run for it when car doors started slamming. The paparazzi had arrived right behind them and were already piling out of their cars.

Raffaelle bit out a curse, then he was wrapping her beneath the hook of a powerful arm.

Cameras flashed. 'Look this way, Elise—!' one of them called out to her.

But she was already being ushered through a pair of doors.

'Keep them out,' Raffaelle instructed the security man manning the foyer.

Before Rachel knew what was happening, he'd marched her into a lift and the doors were closing the two of them inside.

It had happened so fast—all of it—everything! And she'd never felt so afraid in her entire life. Her head was whirling and her legs had gone hollow. The panic had not subsided and it sent the heels of her shoes screeching shrilly beneath her as she spun round, then she lifted an arm and hit out at him with her bag.

He fielded the blow like a man swatting a fly away. 'Calm down,' he gritted.

But Rachel didn't want to calm down. Hair flying about her slender neck as she struggled with him, 'Let me go—let me *go*!' she choked out.

Then she threw back her head and opened her mouth to scream.

Only it didn't arrive. Nothing happened. The

scream remained just a thick lump pulsing in the base of her throat. And he didn't attempt to smother it like he had done outside the hotel but just stood there looking down at her while she stared up at him.

It was crazy—the whole evening had been crazy, but this was *the* craziest part because it felt as if they'd both suddenly been frozen in time.

The panic receded. She forgot to breathe. As far as she could tell, he wasn't breathing either and he was frowning as if he too couldn't understand what was going on.

Gorgeous frown, she found herself thinking. Gorgeous black silk-hooded eyes. In fact he was, she saw as if for the first time, altogether totally breathtaking to look at. His facial bone structure was striking—the high forehead and good cheekbones, the long narrow nose and perfectly symmetrical chin.

And his eyes weren't really grey, but an unusual mixture of green flecked with silver. His skin was amazing, a tightly wrapped casing of honey-gold her fingers remembered with a tense little twitch. The satin-black eyebrows, those luxuriously long eyelashes that were hovering just above the cheekbones, and the mouth…

Don't look at his mouth, she told herself tautly, but she didn't just look, she stared at it. Slender, smooth, slightly parted. The tip of her tongue snaked out to wipe away the now familiar tingle she felt take over her own lips.

He breathed. The warmth of his breath brushed her face, scented with the heady fruits of a rich dark wine. She tried a tense swallow, looked back into his eyes and saw what was coming. He was going to kiss her. Not to stop her screaming or even in anger, but because—

Oh, God, she wanted him to!

He muttered something in Italian. She released the strangest-sounding groan. In the next second he'd captured her mouth and they were kissing— really kissing. Not stolen, fought-for, punishing or smothering kisses, but like two greedy, hungry lovers with a swift, hot, urgent necessity.

Their tongues flickered and slid in a wild, erotic dance of hungry heat. Without caring she was doing it, Rachel lifted her arms up over Raffaelle's shoulders and arched closer until she could feel every inch of him pressing against her, from his hard-packed chest to powerful thighs.

He was so pumped up and solid, his hands moving on a restless journey over the silk dress covering her slender body to the bare flesh of her shoulders, then back down to her small waist again. She became aware that she was purring like a well stroked kitten. He breathed something harsh, then picked her up with his hands and started walking without breaking the kiss.

Her hands were in his hair now, raking his scalp and scrunching its smooth style, the swollen globes of her breasts nudging at him high on his chest.

This should not be happening. This *should not be happening!* a shrill voice screamed inside her head.

The panic returned; Rachel yanked her head back at the same moment that he did the same thing.

Like two people who did not know what the hell was happening to them, they stared at each other again, her eyes wide dark pools of shocked horror and confusion, his blackened by stunned disbelief. Her mouth was burning, her lips still parted and pulsing and swollen as she panted for breath.

He put her down so abruptly she almost toppled off the thin heels of her shoes, her fingers trailing around his shirt collar then down the front of his jacket where they clung, because they had to, to his black satin lapels.

Anger burned now. A thick, dark, intense anger that pulsed from every hard inch of him as he used a key to open a door. Rachel had not noticed that they'd left the lift, never mind crossed another foyer to reach the door!

Manoeuvring them both inside, he kicked the door shut with a foot before peeling her off his front. She staggered dizzily. He walked away down a spacious hallway, then disappeared through another door.

She wanted to faint. She wished she *could* faint. She wished the floor would open up and swallow her whole. Every inch of her body was still alive and buzzing with excitement and a shrill ringing was filling her head.

The ringing stopped abruptly and she blinked. Then she heard his voice ripping out words in sharp Italian and realised the sound had been coming from a phone. She caught Elise's name and reality came tumbling over her like a giant snowball, dousing every bit of heat.

It took real willpower to make her trembling legs walk her down that hallway. But she needed to know what he was saying and to whom he was saying it.

The door was flung wide open on its hinges and she stilled in the opening, staring starkly across a spacious living room with wall-to-wall glass on one side and an expanse of warm wood covering the floor softened by a big creamy-coloured rug. Everything in here was clean-lined and modern. He was standing beside one of several black leather sofas that were carefully placed about the room.

His back was to her. He had a land line telephone clamped to his ear and his hair was still mussed. Her fingers tingled to remind her who had done the mussing. As she continued to stand there, he lifted up a set of long fingers and mussed it up some more.

'Daniella—' he snapped out, then stopped and sighed.

Whatever his stepsister said to him then made his voice alter, the snap going out of it and low, dark, soothing Italian arriving in its place, aimed to apologise and reassure.

Me too, please, Rachel wanted to beg. Reassure me too that this is all just a big nightmare.

But it wasn't and her heart was still beating too fast. The low dark flow of his voice seemed to resonate directly from deep inside his chest before reaching the rolling caress of his tongue.

Oh, God. She put a set of trembling fingers up to cover her eyes. Did all Italian men have deep, sexy voices, or was it just that she had been unlucky enough to meet the only two that could do this to her?

Then an impatient 'Daniella,' arrived again. 'Take my advice and call Gino. Take your bad temper out on him, for I am in no mood to hear this.'

He had switched to English. Rachel dropped her hand in time to watch his shoulders give a tight shrug.

'If *Elise* upstaged you then count your blessings that she was more interesting to the cameras than you and your behaviour were five minutes before!'

Elise…Rachel tensed as a sudden thought hit her. If Raffaelle's stepsister had been fooled tonight into believing she was Elise, then maybe, between them, she and Mark had managed to pull this off!

Rafaelle's voice returned to smooth Italian. Rachel listened intently for the sound of Elise's name being spoken again but it did not happen. A few seconds later he was finishing the call.

Raffaelle put the phone down, then flexed his wide shoulders. He could feel her standing somewhere behind him but he did not want to turn around and find out where.

He did not want to look at her.

He did not know what the hell she was doing to him!

With an impatient yank he undid his bow tie, shifted his stance to angle his body towards the drinks cabinet, then plucked with hard fingers at the top button of his dress shirt as he strode across the room. His jacket came next. He lost it to the back of a sofa. The silence screamed across the gap separating them as he flipped open the cabinet doors and reached for the brandy bottle.

'Drink—?' he offered.

'No thank you,' she huskily declined.

Husky did it. He felt that low sensual voice reach right down inside him and give a hard tug on his loins.

'Keeping a clear head?' he mocked tightly.

'Yes,' she breathed.

Pouring a brandy for himself, he turned with the glass in his hand. She was standing in the doorway in her turquoise dress, with her arms held tensely to her sides. Her hands were gripping the black beaded bag she had tried to hit him with in the lift and her blue eyes were telling him that she was scared.

Some might say that she had asked for everything that was happening to her but Raffaelle was reluctantly prepared to admit that he had been behaving little better than a thug.

He took a sip of his drink, grimly aware that what had broken free in the lift was still busy inside him. He wanted her. He did not know why he wanted her. He'd been tempted by sirens far more adept at their craft than she was without feeling the slightest inclination to give in.

Yet he did—want to give in. In fact the want was now a low-down burning ache in his gut.

She wasn't even what he would call beautiful. Not in the classic Elise-sleek-catwalk-fashion-sense, that was. There again, neither had Elise been catwalk-sleek by the time he'd met her. And this woman's face did not possess the same striking bone structure that Elise had been endowed with. The eyes were the same blue but the nose was different—and the mouth.

The mouth…

Lifting the glass to his lips, Raffaelle half hid his eyes as he studied the mouth, wiped clear of pink lipstick now and still softly swollen from their kiss in the lift. Elise's mouth was a wide classic bow shape whereas this mouth was shaped more evocatively like a heart and was frankly lush. And Elise was taller, though he would hazard a guess the lost inches would not show on a photograph as this one had stretched up and plastered herself against his front.

The dress was expensive—you didn't live most of your life around fashion conscious females without being able to pick out haute couture when you saw it. But it did not fit her. It was too tight in places, like across those two white breasts that were in danger of falling out of it, and it hugged the rounded shape of her slender hips like a second skin.

'Turn round,' he instructed.

She tensed in objection.

'I am looking for your likeness to Elise,' he informed her levelly. 'So humour me and turn around…'

She did. Raffaelle grimaced because he would have been prepared to swear that right now she would rather spit in his face than comply with anything he wanted her to do. The passionate kiss in the lift coming hard on the back of the way she'd looked at him in the car had made her so uptight and defensive he could almost taste her hostility towards him even as she stood there with her back to him.

And that was just another thing about her. Elise

might have been a damn good liar but she had not possessed a single spark of passion or spirit. She'd been quiet and surprisingly shy for someone who had earned her living sashaying along catwalks and posing for glossy magazines.

But that was thinking with hindsight, because he had not known who Elise really was at the time. And he was looking in the wrong place if he expected to find the very married ex-model's nature in a woman who was definitely not her.

The back view did it, though. The back view with the straight hair and the narrow shoulders and tight backside told him exactly why this woman believed she could get away with pretending to be Elise from that angle.

'Had enough?' She spun back to face him so she could fix him with an icy stare.

It made him want to grimace, because if she was allowing herself to believe that such an expression was going to hold him back she was sadly mistaken. Despite the frost, she'd switched him on and now, he discovered, he was not feeling inclined to switch himself off again.

In fact he was beginning to enjoy the sexual sting that was passing between them.

The way he was standing there with his glass

in his hand and his eyes half hidden, he reminded Rachel of a long, lean jungle cat lazily planning the moment when it would pounce.

Still dangerous, in other words.

The loss of his jacket wasn't helping. The bright white of his shirt only made his shoulders look wider and his torso longer and tougher, and the way his loosened bow tie lay in two strips of black either side of his open shirt collar kept on drawing her eyes to the triangle of golden skin at his throat.

Rachel's throat went dry. Oh, please, she begged, will someone get me out of here—?

Because looking at him was recharging the sexual buzz. She could feel it moving through her blood in a slow and sluggishly threatening burn, scary yet exciting—like a war she was having to fight on two fronts.

'Don't you think it is time that you told me your name?'

Rachel tensed, her eyes flicking into focus on his face. Then a strained little laugh broke in her throat because it hadn't occurred to her that he didn't know who she was.

'Rachel,' she pushed out. 'Rachel Carmichael.'

Something about him suddenly altered. For

some unknown reason she felt as if the air circulating around him had gone as tense as a cracked whip. And the eyes—the eyes were not merely hooded now, they'd narrowed into sharp eyelash-framed slits.

'Well, hello, Rachel Carmichael,' he drawled in a very slow, lazy tone that made the hairs on the back of her neck stand on end. 'Now this has just become very interesting…'

'Why has it?' she asked warily.

'Why don't you come and sit down so we can talk about it?'

She had the impression that the jungle cat in him had just sharpened its teeth. Taut as a bow string and balanced right on the balls of her feet now, Rachel wondered if this would be a good time to try to make a run for it.

But the idea lasted for only a moment. He had not brought her up here to his apartment to let her get away before she had given him an explanation as to why she'd set him up tonight.

Making herself walk across the room took courage, especially when he watched her all the way as if she was performing some special provocative act designed purposely to keep his attention engaged.

Oh, God, did he have to look so sleekly at ease and so gorgeously interested?

Beginning to feel disturbingly hollow from the neck down, if she did not count the sparking sting making itself felt, Rachel picked one of the black sofas at random and sat down right on its edge.

The skirt to her dress immediately rode upwards to reveal more slender thigh than was decent with a peek of her stocking lace tops. Unclipping her fingers from the death grip they had on her bag she gave a tug at the dress's hem, only to notice to her horror that its bodice wasn't doing much to keep her modesty covered, either.

And still he stood there watching her every single move, deliberately, she suspected, building on the sexual tension that was fizzing in the air. Her heart was pounding. She refused to look up. She wanted to swallow but would not allow herself the luxury of trying to shift the anxious lump lodged in her throat.

Then he moved and she jerked up her head, unable to stop the wary response, only to feel almost dizzy with embarrassment when she saw how he was looking at her.

'I will have that drink now,' she burst out, desperate for him to turn away so she could pull up the bodice of her dress without him watching.

One of those sleek black eyebrows arched in quizzing mockery at her abrupt change of mind about the drink. He knew what she was trying to do. It was scored into his eyes and his body language.

'What would you like?' he asked politely.

'I don't know—anything,' she shook out.

He turned his back. Rachel feathered out a tense breath and hurriedly rearranged herself. In all her life she had never felt so out of sorts and out of place as she was feeling right now, sitting on this sofa, wearing this dress, with that man standing only a few feet away.

She was nobody's luxury appendage—never had been. She'd always left that kind of thing to the more beautiful and capable Elise. Playing the role given to her tonight had been tough on her pride, from the moment she'd donned the whole image. And the only man she'd ever thrown herself at in her whole life before tonight had been Alonso, and, she recalled with a grimace, he'd been more or less crawling all over her by then anyway.

And Alonso hadn't been rich. He'd just been a very junior car salesman with good lines in smart suits and a tiny apartment. He drove flashy cars but he didn't own them, and he'd earned less money than she had earned picking fruit on a farm just outside Naples.

A glass appeared in front of her. Glancing up, she unclipped one of her hands from her bag and took it with a mumbled, 'Thanks,' then sat staring at it wondering what the heck was in it?

'Splash of vodka topped up with tonic,' he provided the answer. 'And it is not spiked with something lethal, if that is what the frown is about.'

'I wasn't—'

'Then you should,' he intruded curtly. 'You don't know me, Rachel Carmichael. I might go in for drug-enhanced love-ins. How old are you, by the way?'

Rachel blinked. 'Twenty-three. Why, what has my age got to do with anything?'

'Just curious.' He sat down right next to her sending her spine arching into a defensive stretch.

Raffaelle saw it happen and smiled. The air circulating around them was alive with an ever increasing sting of awareness. He could feel it. He knew that she could feel it. What he could not figure out was *why* it was there and what he was going to do about it.

Liar, the dry part of his brain fed back.

'Okay…' Relaxing into the sofa, he stretched out his long legs. 'Now, start talking.'

Talking… Sending her tongue round her dry lips, Rachel looked down at the bag she was still clutching in one hand and made a small shift of her wrist so she could see the time on her watch.

It was just coming up to midnight. How long did Mark need to do his thing with his digital camera, write his accompanying piece, then file it with the newspaper via the Internet?

She looked at her bag with the comforting feel of her cellphone inside it, and wondered if she dared take it out and ring him to check?

Great idea, she then thought heavily. As if Raffaelle Villani was going to let her contact anyone until he had his explanation.

'Sit back and relax,' he invited.

What she did was stiffen up all the more. 'I'm perfectly relaxed as I am, thank you.'

'No, you are not. There is tension—here…' A finger arrived in the naked taut hollow between her shoulders, sending her spine into another muscle splitting arch as if she'd been stung by an electric shock.

The sensation flung her, gasping to her feet. 'That wasn't—necessary,' she protested.

'You think not?'

'No.' Taking a few shaky steps away from him, she put the glass to her mouth and sipped while he watched her through half hidden eyes and a knowing smile on his lips.

'We share chemistry, *cara*.'

Rachel laughed thickly. 'That of kidnapper and victim.'

'And who do you believe is the victim here—?'

Just like that, with one smooth question, he brought the whole madness which had made up this evening tumbling down to where it really belonged.

For which of them was the real victim? Certainly not her, she had to admit. He had every right to be angry. She had no right to be anything at all.

On the short sigh that quivered as it left her, Rachel finally took responsibility for her own misdemeanours. It was no use trying to pretend she was innocent when she wasn't. Or to wish Raffaelle Villani a million miles away because he'd ruined all their plans when he had stopped her from getting away back there at the hotel.

He was right about the chemistry too. Just turning to look at his long, lean, relaxed sprawl, giving off all kinds of innate sexual messages, sent her insides into an instant tight spiral spin.

Then—okay, she told herself grimly, let's keep this strictly to business, then maybe the—other—stuff will die a natural death.

On that stern piece of good common sense, she lifted her chin, pushed her eyes upwards to fix them on his face, then she steadied her breathing and plunged right in.

'As I just told you, my name is Rachel Carmichael,' she reminded him. 'Elise is my half-sister. W-we had different fathers, hence the different surnames…'

CHAPTER THREE

HE DID not move. He remained relaxed. His eyes told her absolutely nothing and his mouth held on to its smooth flat line.

So why did Rachel get the unnerving impression that he had already worked most of that out?

'Elise has been out of the modelling scene for over five years now since—since she married Leo Savakis—'

'And gave him a son.'

Rachel could only nod, pressing her lips together as she did so, because she knew without him adding that dry comment, how badly all of this reflected on Elise.

'Leo is an…awesome guy,' she continued. 'He is the very hands-on head of the Savakis shipping empire as well as being a respected international lawyer, expert in British, Greek and American corporate law—'

'Skip the CV. I know about Leo Savakis,' he coolly cut in.

Of course he would know about Leo. Most people who moved in high business circles would have heard about her brother-in-law's remarkable career.

'He's a very busy man.'

'Aren't we all?' drawled this high mover—in the business world at least.

'S-sometimes Elise feels—neglected.'

'Ah,' he sighed. 'So I am to get the sob story before you lurch into the ugly part.'

'Don't mock what you have never suffered, Mr Villani!' Rachel flared up in her sister's defence. 'When you've gone from being the face on every glossy magazine to a stay-at-home wife and mother with no identity to call your own, then you might begin to understand!'

He didn't even bother to respond to that heated outburst. 'So she feels—neglected...' he prompted instead.

'And lonely.' Once again Rachel steadied her breathing. 'When Leo works abroad he prefers Elise to stay put in London or on his island in Greece. He says it's all to do with security,' she explained. 'He's made enemies in his line of work and...'

'Naturally feels the need to protect his wife and his son.'

'Wouldn't you?' Rachel flashed.

He raised a black satin eyebrow. 'Are you working in defence of Mr Savakis here or his poor neglected wife?'

'Both,' Rachel declared loyally. 'I *like* Leo…'

But she wouldn't want him as a husband, she added silently. He was too overwhelmingly unreadable and dauntingly self-controlled. He adored Elise though, she was certain of it. It was just that…

'He's been virtually living in Chicago for the last twelve months, working on a high-profile case that only allows him back home for the occasional flying visit.'

'Hence poor Elise feeling lonely and neglected—'

'If you don't stop being nasty about her, I'm going to leave!'

He shifted his shoulders against the black leather, then moved his legs, bending them out of their lazy sprawl so he could rest one ankle on the other knee. Rachel's eyes were drawn to the lean bowl between his hipbones where the expensive black fabric of his trousers sat easily against—

Oh, please, someone help me! she thought despairingly and wanted to run away again.

He moved a hand next, lifting it up so he could stroke a long finger across the flat line of his lips. Above the stroking finger, his grey-green eyes feathered a ponderous look over her in a way that further fanned the sexual charge.

Did all Italian men have an ability to seduce just by using body language, or was it just her misfortune that they affected *her* like this?

Disturbed by the whole hectic physical war going on here, Rachel put some distance between them by walking across the room to stand staring out of one of the huge plate glass windows. London—the River Thames, Westminster and Tower Bridge—lay spanned out before her in a familiar night scene.

Behind her his silent study pin-pricked her spine.

He had not even bothered to challenge her threat to leave. It was as if he knew she was becoming more and more trapped here by the sexual pull and he was enjoying feeding it.

One of the friends she'd made during her stay in Naples had once claimed that Italian men could seduce you and make you feel wonderful about falling in love with them without so much as considering falling in love themselves. It was the

Italian way. Apparently you were supposed to feel blessed that they'd bothered to notice you at all.

Because they were conceited and arrogant by nature, so confident in their prowess as mighty lovers, that the suggestion that they might not assuage your every sexual fantasy never entered their minds or their beds. Such an uncrushable self-belief was seductive in itself. Rachel had fallen for it with Alonso. Now here she was, feeling the pull again and with a much more dangerous beast than Alonso ever had been.

It was time to put it to death, she told herself.

Turning from the window, she looked back at him. 'Leo knows about your affair with Elise,' she announced.

And saw death happen to sexual promise as he flicked those eyes into sharp focus on her face.

'He was sent photographs of the two of you together in a restaurant here in London, then later being very intimate on a dance floor,' she pushed on.

His tight curse brought him to his feet.

'Elise got upset—'

'Naturally,' he gritted.

Rachel bit down hard on her lower lip. 'She denied everything, which was a bit stupid when

Leo was standing there with the photographic evidence,' she allowed. 'F-fortunately the photos were dark and very grainy and she insisted that the blonde in them could be anyone.'

'She lied, in other words.'

'Wouldn't you have done in her place?'

His dark head went back. 'If I was so miserable in my marriage that I needed to look elsewhere for—company, I would be man enough to say so *before* the event!'

'Well, good for you, Mr Villani,' Rachel commended. 'It must be really great to be so sure of yourself that you *know* what you would do in any given situation! Well, Elise *lied*,' she stressed. 'And, right off the top of her head, she suggested that the woman in the photos could even be me. Leo wasn't impressed—I don't normally look or dress like this, you see—'

He flicked her a cynical look. 'Another liar in the family, then.'

'Yes,' Rachel sighed, seeing no use in denying it. 'I had been staying with Elise in London for a while to—to keep her company while Leo was away. She was so low and depressed I encouraged her to go out with an old f-friend from her modelling days and—and enjoy life a bit instead of moping around the house waiting for…' She stopped, shutting the rest of that away where it belonged.

By his expression she knew he knew what she meant.

'Anyway,' she went on after a moment. 'She took me up on the offer and really started to cheer up and be her old self! But I had no idea she was out there enjoying herself with another man…'

'Oh, call it as it is, *cara*, we had the hots for each other.'

'You don't need to be so crude about it!' she said heatedly.

'What happened next?' He was striding across the room towards the brandy bottle to replenish his empty glass and there was nothing languid in his movements now.

'Elise told Leo that *I* had been seeing someone while I was staying with her…'

'A someone who just happened to be me—?' Brandy splashed into the glass.

Rachel watched it and mentally crossed her fingers and hoped he had the steady head for it. 'She was fighting for her marriage.'

He swallowed the drink. 'So did Savakis call you up to demand confirmation and you lied to him for your sister's sake?'

'Leo didn't do anything.' Ignoring his sarcasm, she kept strictly to the point. 'Instead he chose to let the subject drop.'

'Generous man,' he drawled. 'Or a sadly besotted one.'

The idea of Leo being either generous or besotted was so alien to Rachel that she had to stop and think about it and still couldn't get either scenario to fit the Leo she knew.

'Things have been—strained between the two of them ever since, and now...' Rachel gathered herself in before she revealed the next bit. 'Elise has just found out that she's pregnant.'

Raffaelle responded to this with an abrupt stiffening of his long body. The glass clenched between his fingers, he turned a narrowed look on her face.

'Do go on,' he invited softly.

Rachel wished she didn't have to go on but she knew that she did. 'W-with the timing and—everything, there's a big chance that Leo might not believe the baby is his.'

'You mean he does not know about it yet?'

'Not yet,' Rachel murmured.

'And is it his baby?'

'Yes!' she cried out. 'Unless you are wondering if it might be your baby?' she then could not resist hitting back.

'I know it isn't.' His mouth was as hard now as his eyes were like ice.

Rachel shivered. 'It's Leo's baby,' she repeated firmly. 'Conceived during one of his flying visits home. He'd only been there one night when he was telling Elise over the breakfast table that he was flying back to Chicago the next day. S-so she rebelled at his arrogant assumption that he could just fly in and—' The rest was cut off and smothered. But once again she knew that he knew what she was getting at. 'So Elise decided to punish him by telling him she had started her period and so was off limits...'

Because, as Elise had said, if Leo thought he could fly in just to ease his libido, then he could go back to Chicago and to libido hell!

'*Dio*,' Raffaelle muttered. 'The sly machinations of a selfish woman never cease to impress me.'

'Nor am I impressed by the casual attitude of a man on the hunt for sex!'

'Was that remark aimed at me?' he demanded.

'Does it fit?' Rachel lanced back. 'Did you or did you not hit on my sister because you fancied your chances in her bed?'

Guilty as charged. His teeth came together. 'I did not know that she was married,' he declared stiffly.

'And that's your excuse?' Rachel denounced. 'Why didn't you know she was married?' she demanded. 'She was a famous ex-model, for goodness' sake! Her face used to be seen everywhere. Her marriage made the front pages of every glossy there is!'

'Does she look like the famous model any more?' he hit back. 'You know she does not! She carries more weight now and her face has altered. And she did not exactly go out of her way to tell me who she was!'

'What did she do then—pretend to be Catwoman, complete with rubber mask?'

Rachel saw him make a grab at his temper. 'She used a different name,' he said.

A different name—? That was one small detail Elise had left out of her account of her reckless rebellion against Leo.

'What name—?' She frowned at him.

He looked at her, then dared to laugh, though it wasn't a very pleasant-sounding laugh. 'Does—*Rachel Carmichael* mean much to you?'

Rachel suddenly needed to sit down again. Walking on trembling legs to the nearest sofa, she

sank into its soft black leather and put the glass
to her equally trembling mouth.

'I see you recognise the name,' he drawled hate-
fully.

'Shut up!' she whipped back; she was trying to
think.

The devious witch, the calculating madam!
She'd gone out there on the town stuffed full of
rebellion, using *her* name as a cover-up, while in-
sisting that Leo's precious security guards
remained at the house to guard her son!

'No wonder Mark dragged me back here,' she
mumbled.

'Who the hell is Mark?' Raffaelle Villani
rapped out.

'My half-brother—the one with the camera,'
she enlightened.

'You mean you are related to one of the paparazzi?'

Rachel shifted uncomfortably. 'Mark and Elise
are twins.'

He didn't bother to say anything to that, but just
stood there glaring into space. The atmosphere
was pretty much too thick to breathe now and
Rachel was wishing she was wearing armour

plating because she had a horrible feeling she was going to need it soon.

'From where?' he demanded suddenly.

Looking up at him, she just blinked.

'You said that your brother dragged you back,' he enlightened her. 'From where—?'

'Oh—Devon,' Rachel responded. 'I work there on the family farm—organic,' she added for no reason she could think of.

His raking scan of her was downright incredulous. 'You…are a *farmer*?'

Her chin shot up. 'What's the matter with that, Mr Villani?' she challenged. 'Does it bruise your precious ego to know you're about to be intimately linked to a poor farming girl instead of some rich chick with a three-hundred-year-old pedigree—?'

Silence clattered—no, it thundered down as both of them realised at the same time what it was she had just said.

'"Intimately linked—?"' he fed into that rumbling thunder.

Rachel bit down hard on her bottom lip to stop it from quivering. The thickened air in the room began to curdle—or was it the vodka she wasn't used to drinking that was beginning to make her feel slightly sick?

'Explain that,' he raked out.

'I w-will in a minute,' she whispered. 'I just need to—get my head together to...' say what still had not been said.

Abandoning what was left of the glass of vodka and her bag to the floor at her feet, she made herself stand up again, preferring to meet what was about to come back at her from an upright position with her hands free rather than have him loom over her like a threatening thunderclap.

Why did he have to be so intimidatingly tall and big?

She found herself sending him a plea for understanding with her eyes as she lurched back into speech. 'Elise provided this d-dress and the invitation to the charity thing tonight,' she explained. 'Then she was packed off to Chicago with her son this afternoon f-for a surprise visit to Leo, while Mark and I...'

'Set up the sting on me?'

Pressing her lips together, she nodded, deciding not to object to the latest label he'd hung on them because it was the truth, and there was still more to come.

'Tomorrow morning you and I will appear together in a Sunday tabloid—'

'Saying what—?' he bit out.

Oh, God, she groaned silently. 'S-something like—Raffaelle Villani goes public with his latest w-woman…'

Having to really bite down hard on her bottom lip now, Rachel searched the hard angles of his face for a small sign that he wasn't into murder—but she didn't see it.

'It was important to convince Leo that the woman in the photographs he has in his possession and the one who will appear in tomorrow's paper are the same person and *cannot* be Elise if she is in Chicago with him!'

And that was the bottom line.

Suddenly he was a tall dark stranger standing there. A man so cold and so very still it was as if he had pulled on the same awesome cloak of implacability that Leo always wore.

The silence gnawed. So did the heightened tension which began sapping the defences that had kept Rachel going through all of this.

'It should have ended there,' she pushed into the taut atmosphere. 'If you had behaved as predicted and let me get away from you, I would have disappeared back to Devon and tomorrow's tabloid spread would have become Monday's bin liner—

over and forgotten about—and my sister's marriage would have been safe!'

It was the way it worked, Mark had said. Raffaelle Villani would have no case to deny. He might bluster and demand a retraction from the paper but that would be all he could do. Elise's name would not be mentioned by Mark and other than Leo receiving hard evidence that his wife was not the woman in the grainy photographs with Raffaelle Villani, everything else would just—go away.

But this man had not reacted as predicted. He'd grabbed and held on to her. And the pap-pack had caught their scent. Now she was stuck here in his apartment with the pack no doubt waiting outside ready to pounce on her the moment that she tried to leave.

And where was her darling quick thinking half-brother? Putting his twin's needs first, as he always did.

Now Rachel hadn't a clue as to where it was all going to go from here except—

It was time to beg, she recognised starkly. Time to appeal to one very cold and angry Raffaelle Villani for his understanding and co-operation, when deep down she knew they deserved neither.

She moved towards him. 'Mr Villani,' she murmured huskily, 'please, just think about it. I was actually doing you a favour too tonight because if Leo—'

'What the hell is—*this*?'

Rachel hadn't realised she'd lifted a hand out towards him in appeal until his long fingers were suddenly clamped around her wrist.

'W-what—?' she said jerkily.

Grim mouth flattening, he lifted up her hand until her fingers dangled in front of her confused face. She had to blink twice to focus on the diamond-encrusted sapphire ring twinkling back at her.

'Oh,' she said and swallowed. She'd forgotten all about the ring.

'You are betrothed—?' he enquired with blistering thinness.

'N-no.' Rachel shook her head. 'It—it's nothing; the ring is a f-fake, just w-window-dressing.'

'Window-dressing,' he repeated.

'Part of the look…' She was beginning to squirm inside again. 'Leo needed to see it if he was going to…'

'Believe you were not his wife?'

She nodded, then swallowed again. 'Elise's engagement ring is a big single yellow diamond. Th-this one is so glaringly different that it…'

Her voice trailed away, the hiss of his breath making it do so because she knew he had caught on.

'So, let me see if I have this clear,' he said grimly. 'You dressed yourself up to look like your half-sister—from behind, then you threw yourself at my neck, kissing me as if I am your…?'

He wanted her to say it. Her heart began thumping. He was going to make her confess the final full duplicity.

'L-lover,' she breathed.

'*Betrothed* lover?' His voice was getting softer by the second.

Rachel licked her lips and nodded.

'And I was not supposed to issue an instant denial about this?'

'Th-there's a letter going to be h-hand-delivered here to you tomorrow along with the relevant newspaper,' she told him shakily. 'The letter will explain everything we have talked about and point out to you that to expose the photograph as a lie will leave you open to questions about wh-whose baby it is Elise is carrying.'

'*Madre de Dio*,' he breathed. 'You are truly devious.'

He was right and she was, but— 'This is serious, Mr Villani!' she cried out. 'You don't know Leo! He's one hell of a strict Greek! He's also an absolute killer expert on law! If he decides that his wife has been cheating on him with you and could be having *your* baby…for all your wealth and power, he will drag you to the courtroom and through the gutters along with Elise!'

He threw her hand away. 'I never touched her—!' he bit out angrily.

'Even this very trusting sister can't believe that!'

Her denunciation bounced off the walls and the sheets of plate glass while the air sizzled with his undiluted rage.

'One kiss, Mr Villani,' Rachel stressed urgently. 'One small kiss stolen from the wife of Leo Savakis and he will never forgive her, and you will find yourself stuck with the worst kind of enemy there is!'

He just turned and walked off, striding across the expanse of wood flooring and out through the door.

Rachel followed, quivering, shaken to the roots because it was only now, when faced with what this all meant to *him*, that she was beginning to realise how none of them had given much thought to how unfairly they were treating him in all of this.

She hurried after him. 'I'm so sorry…'

The husky quaver of her apology fell on stony ground. It had been such a useless thing to say anyway, so she didn't blame him for the filthy comment he threw back at her, as one of his arms flew out with an angry hand attached to it, which hit open another door to allow him to keep walking without altering his angry stride.

Rachel found herself coming to a trembling halt in yet another doorway. This one opened on to a shiny black and white kitchen and he was standing by a huge black mirror fronted fridge. One of the doors was swinging open, but by the way he was just staring Rachel received the pained impression that he didn't know what it was he was staring into.

'Please believe me when I say I did *try* to explain it all to you earlier—at the charity thing!' she tried again—frantically. 'I *insisted* to Mark that we should at least attempt to get your understanding and cooperation but…' she sucked in a breath '…you wouldn't give me the chance to speak and then the whole thing j-just ran out of control!'

He slammed the fridge door shut and turned to face her. If her trembling legs would have let her, Rachel knew she would be running by now.

But—look at him, she told herself helplessly as he began striding towards her. He was so gloriously magnificent in his anger, his face muscles stretched tight across his amazing bone structure and his torso pumped up like a warrior about to begin a slaying-fest.

He reached for her.

She quivered. 'Y-you—'

He shut her up with his hard hot mouth to mouth that totally blacked out her brain. When he let her up for air again she was dizzy and disorientated, in no fit state to find herself being dragged by the hand down the hallway then out of the door to the lift.

His free hand stabbed the call button. Bright balls of panic spun in her head. He was going to throw her out. He was going to hand her to the wolves out there and—

'Please don't do this,' she begged him on the very—very edge of tears now.

He pulled her into the lift. They rode down with him standing there in front of her, with her wrist still his prisoner and the rest of her pinned against the lift wall by the steely glitter in his eyes.

'Think about it,' she begged unsteadily. 'You don't want to—'

He swooped and cut the words off the ruthless way, with another open mouthed onslaught that lost her the will to even stand.

But she had to stand. She had to follow where he pulled as they left the lift and crossed the foyer with a curious security guard looking on. Then a hard hand pushed open the main doors and Rachel lost the next few seconds beneath the glare of flashing flickering lights and the pandemonium of questions that burst out.

His arm was around her shoulders now, hugging her to him and keeping her upright.

'Smile,' he hissed and she smiled like an alien.

Then the words came, those low, smooth accented tones dryly confirming that no, as they could see, she was not Elise. She was in fact Elise's beautiful half-sister, Rachel Carmichael.

Then he let drop the big one, by calmly inviting their congratulations because they had just become engaged to be married.

The fake ring was displayed on her finger for the pack to snap to their greedy hearts' content.

How long had they known each other? Where had they met?

He answered all the questions with the relaxed humour of one who had all the answers, since he was merely duplicating facts from his short affair with Elise.

Breathing took on a shallow necessity aimed to maintain the fragile beat of her heart. The rest was a haze, a fog of nothing in which she must have performed well because no one suggested she was about to pass out or, worse, that she looked more like a horrified prisoner being hauled to the gallows than a happily betrothed future bride.

'Now you have what you came for would it be possible that you can do us a favour and leave us in peace?'

So lightly requested, so full of lazy charm. The pack laughed. He turned her within the iron grip of his arm. Silence hit with a deafening force as the doors closed with them back inside.

'Congratulations, Mr Villani, Miss Carmichael,' the eavesdropping security guard said with a grin.

If the man holding her clamped to his side said anything in response then Rachel didn't hear it. She was too busy trying to decide if she was dizzy with relief because he hadn't thrown her out there to face the paparazzi alone, or if she was dizzy with fear over what was still to come.

They travelled back up in the lift. She was in

shock. She had been totally incapacitated by a man locked into his own agenda. An agenda that involved him seizing control of a situation they— *she* had taken away from him.

His apartment door closed behind them. Rachel shivered. And still the ordeal did not end there. The arm propelled her down the hall and in through another door. *It* closed with a quiet deathly click and only then did she manage to find the strength to break free.

She had moved three shaky steps before it hit her that this was a bedroom. A very male bedroom with very masculine items scattered around it and a very large bed standing out like a threat, with its very dark plum-coloured linen upon which it was too easy to imprint the solid frame of a dark-haired honey-skinned man.

She turned. He was still by the door and watching her. Not one small gram of anger had softened from his face. Her skin gave a fizz of alarm-cum-excitement because, even in anger, the way he was looking at her was stripping her bare to her quivering skin.

'Why—?' she breathed.

'You wanted my co-operation and you have had it,' he answered. 'Now I want what I want, and you, Miss Carmichael, are about to pay your dues.'

He started closing the gap between them.

'No.' Rachel shook her head and began backing away. 'I won't let you do this.'

'Oh come on, *mi amore*,' he taunted coldly. 'We are betrothed to be married. You wear my ring on your finger and my impeccably mannered family is going to try not to be shocked that my bride is wearing farmers' boots to her wedding and straw to decorate her hair.'

'Very funny,' she muttered, looking about her for an escape.

'They will tread daintily between organic lettuce and—'

'Will you just stop this!' His words might taunt but the rest was now getting scary. 'Look,' she said quickly. 'I know you are angry—and I know that you have every right to be.'

'*Grazie.*'

'Oh, God,' she choked as his hands closed around her waist and the shock of feeling them there again lit up her skin. 'I'm *sorry* about *everything,* okay?'

His dark head began to lower. Rachel tried to arch away.

'Your heart is racing.'

'Because you're *frightening* me!'

'Or exciting you.'

No, frightening—*frightening me!* Rachel repeated—though only inside her head where a strange tumbling darkness was gathering, closing around her like a cold mist that began to take her legs from beneath her and brought forth a string of soft tight curses as she began to go limp.

CHAPTER FOUR

SHE came around to find she was lying on the bed and her head was pounding. Someone moved close by and she flicked open her eyes as Raffaelle Villani came to lean over her.

With a startled jerk she tried to get up but he pushed her back down again.

'Be calm,' he said grimly. 'I do not ravish helpless females.'

Well, forgive me for not believing you, she wanted to say but, 'W-what happened to me?' she whispered instead.

'You—fainted.' His mouth tightened as he said that and his eyes were hooded; in fact his whole face was hidden behind a tightly controlled mask that did not make Rachel feel any safer. 'You are also very cold.'

It was only as a soft cashmere throw landed across her that she realised she was shivering.

'I should not have taken you outside to meet the press wearing only that dress.'

The press. It all came flooding back like a recurring nightmare and she closed her eyes again. 'I can't believe you actually did that,' she whispered unsteadily.

Straightening up, *'Mi dispiace,'* he offered stiffly. 'I have no excuse for frightening you as badly as I did.'

'I wasn't talking about you playing the sex maniac!' She sat up and this time he did not stop her. 'I meant what you just did down there in front of all those reporters.' She grabbed her dizzy forehead and stared up at him. 'Have you *no* idea what it is you've done?'

'I did what I had to do,' he stated coldly.

'Great,' she choked. 'You did what you had to do and managed to escalate this whole thing right out of control!'

'It was out of control long before I became involved. You said as much yourself.'

So she had. 'Well, we are now stuck with a fake betrothal, complete with a fake ring and all the other fake stuff that is going to come with it.'

'But your sister's marriage will be safe, which,

of course, makes the subterfuge, sacrifice and lies worth it?'

The sarcasm was still alive if the frightening anger had lessened, Rachel heard, and went to get up.

'Stay there,' he commanded, turning to stride towards the door. 'Give yourself chance to—warm up a little and—recover.'

Recover for what? Rachel wondered half hysterically. She was never going to recover from this awful night for as long as she lived!

Ignoring his command, she moved to sit on the edge of the bed, then sat trying to calm the sickly swimming sensation still taking place in her head.

'I have to find a way to get out of here undetected so I can go home,' she mumbled, more to herself than to him.

Still, he heard it and paused at the door. 'Where is home when you are in London?'

Usually with Elise but, 'With Mark, right now,' she replied, then squinted a look at her watch. 'He will be worrying where I am.'

'Not so I noticed, *cara*,' he drawled cynically. 'Not that it matters,' he then dismissed, 'because from now on you will be living right here with me.'

'I will not!' she gasped out.

He had the door open now. 'If my freedom to

choose what I do with my life has been curtailed, then so has yours,' he declared. 'So, until we find a way out of this situation which does not involve *my* loss of face, you and I, Miss Carmichael, will in effect be stuck to each other with glue. So lie down again and get used to it.'

With that he walked out, leaving Rachel gaping at the empty space he'd last filled with his cold anger, which was just as bad as the hot anger from before!

'But that's just stupid—!' she fired after him. 'Betrothed people don't have to live together!'

If he heard her he did not come back to argue and, after a second, Rachel slumped her shoulders where she sat, wondering dully if he didn't have a point. Now the press wagon was rolling, nothing was going to stop it in the near future without someone—or all of them—losing face.

She closed her eyes, wishing her head would just stop spinning now so she could think.

She needed to ring Mark. The whole story had gone bottom upwards and she needed to warn him then get his take on what she should do next.

Ignoring the swimming room, she got up then just stood looking down at her feet. Her shoes had disappeared. Tugging the throw around her chilled shoulders, she began searching for them but they weren't anywhere to be found.

He must have taken them with him. To stop her from making a bid for freedom? He had to be crazy if he thought her mad enough to run out there where the paparazzi waited—with or without her shoes!

She did find a bathroom, though, which she was sincerely glad about, since she had not been near one for hours and hours. It smelled of Raffaelle Villani: clean and tangy, with a hint of spice.

Nice, she thought as she washed her hands in the basin. The kind of expensive scents you expected to surround a super-elite male. Then she supposed she must also smell super-elite right now, bearing in mind that her body had been pampered by a whole range of expensive products Elise had provided along with the expensive hair-style and dress.

She caught sight of herself in the bathroom mirror then and was actually taken aback because she hardly recognised herself—that sleek blonde thing with dead straight hair and heavy make-up.

Well, she thought grimly as she viewed the thick licks of mascara that lengthened her eyelashes and made her eyes look bluer than they really were, everyone just loved to tell her that she had the potential to look almost as good as Elise if she'd only take time with her appearance. Now it seemed they'd achieved their dearest wish, only—

She was not and had never wanted to be Elise, had she? And that person she could see in the mirror was just someone pretending to be something she was not.

The fraud, in other words—the fake.

The pink lipstick had all gone by now, she saw, but her lips still looked fuller than she was used to seeing them. Fuller and sexier because of too many hot kisses shared with a complete stranger.

A stranger who was in for a big shock when he eventually got to meet the real Rachel Carmichael.

Releasing a sigh, she turned away from the mirror and went back into the bedroom to search for that other item that had gone missing—her bag with her cellphone inside it.

It wasn't in the bedroom so she let herself into the hallway, then walked down it and into the living room. The dress did not feel so indecently short now that her ankles were no longer elevated by four-inch heels, she noticed as she walked.

She heard the bag before she found it because

her phone was already ringing. It had to be Mark—who else? she mocked grimly as she followed the sound and found the bag lying on the floor by the sofa she'd last sat down upon.

Her half-finished glass of vodka stood along-side it. As she bent to get her bag there was a moment when she considered picking up the glass first and downing what was left in true Dutch courage style before she told Mark what had happened.

In the end she didn't need to tell him. Pushing her hair behind her ear, she put the phone to it.

'Rachel, what the hell are you doing in Raffaelle Villani's apartment?' Mark's voice all but pounced.

'How did you find out where I am—?' she asked.

'Because it's all over the bloody Internet!'

A sound from behind her made her turn to find Raffaelle Villani propping up the living room doorway. His shirt sleeves were rolled up now, re-vealing tanned muscular forearms sprinkled with just enough dark hair to make her wonder where else on his body it might be.

Her stomach muscles quivered. Her mouth went dry. Fluttering down her eyelashes, 'It's nothing for you to panic about,' she said huskily into the phone. 'I—I've been explaining the—

situation to R-Raffaelle.' The name fell uneasily from her lips and she caught the way one of his eyebrows arched in mocking note of that. 'He—he's being very understanding about it as—as I told you and Elise he would be once he'd heard all the facts.'

There was a short silence. 'I'm coming to get you.'

'No—!' Rachel pushed out. 'It—it's better that you stay away from here.'

'Because I'm the press? Because between the two of you—you've come up with this crazy engagement announcement that is flying round Europe as we speak?'

That far, that quickly—? Rachel swallowed.

'I'm your brother first, Rachel,' Mark was saying angrily. 'And if that bastard is—'

'Well, it's just a bit too late to remember that, Mark!' she cut in. 'After the way you left me standing tonight, I wish I didn't have a brother!'

'I thought you were right behind me until I reached my car.' He had the grace to sound uncomfortable. 'When I did think to look back, the rest of my cronies were piling out of the hotel and I couldn't see you anywhere, so I assumed you'd disappeared in the other direction.'

'And, happy with that very stupid idea, you just went home without me to post your scoop.' Wasn't that just typically Mark?

'I had a deadline,' he grunted.

I had a *life*, Rachel thought angrily. 'Well, it's too late to come at me with the brotherly concern now.'

'Yeah, you're right.' He sighed. 'Sorry, Rachel. So he's okay with all of this, then?'

Straight from apology back to business, Rachel noticed. 'Yes,' she said.

He sucked in a breath. 'So when are you coming back here?'

'Coming back?' She looked at Raffaelle Villani. He was standing there, waiting to hear her answer as much as Mark was.

And she knew suddenly that she was going nowhere. She owed it to this man to play the game the way he had decided it would be played.

'I'm not coming back,' she said to Mark, but it was this other man's wry tilt of his dark head that held her attention. 'We—we're still talking through our options,' she added. 'So I'm staying here f-for now.'

'Just talking?' Mark asked silkily.

She couldn't answer, not straight away anyway, because there was something about the way Raffaelle was looking at her now that—

'Yes,' she said.

But the gap had been too long for her street-wise, cynical half-brother. She heard him let out a long breath of air. 'I hope you know what you're doing,' he said grimly. 'He isn't the kind of man you want to become mixed up with.'

Great advice, she thought, after the event. 'I'll call you—tomorrow,' was all she said.

'I had better go and ring Elise to tell her she can stop worrying.'

And that was Mark, Rachel noted bleakly, back to prioritizing in his usual way—his twin always being a bigger priority for him than she ever could be.

'Okay,' she murmured. 'Tell her I—'

'Great,' he cut in. 'Got to go now, Rachel. I need to change my copy before it goes to print. Do you have any idea how much you've messed me about by making that announcement tonight?'

The phone went dead. Rachel stared at it. And, for the first time since this whole wretched evening began, she felt the thick push of weak tears hit her eyes and her throat.

Raffaelle watched as she continued to stand there with the cellphone in her hand. She'd gone pale again and if her body language was speaking to him then it was telling him that she had just been tossed aside like a used bloody pawn.

Anger pumped at his chest. He wanted to kick something—her twin siblings, for instance.

'What did you expect?' he demanded brusquely. 'A full rescue, complete with armour and swords? You are not the main player on this chessboard, *cara*—Elise is.'

'I know that,' she whispered and sank down on to the sofa.

He breathed out a sigh. 'At least her unborn child will get to know its rightful father.'

He'd meant that to sound comforting but it had come out sounding harsh. She winced, pressing her lips together and dipping her head. Her hair slid forward, revealing the vulnerable curve of her slender white nape.

Raffaelle brought his teeth together, his tongue sitting behind them and tingling with a mixed-up desire to taste what he could see and the knowledge that it was at real risk of being bitten off if he did not take more care about what he said.

With a reluctance to let his mood soften, he pushed himself away from the door and walked towards her. She heard him coming and stiffened her spine. When he leant down with the intention of picking up her glass to offer it to her, she actually shuddered.

'Please don't start dragging me around again,' she choked out.

Was that what he had been doing—?

Yes, that was what he had been doing, Raffaelle realised, and straightened up with a jerk. 'I'm—sorry,' he said.

'Everyone is sorry.' She laughed tensely. 'Doesn't help much though, does it?'

He couldn't argue with that so he threw himself down on the sofa beside her and released another sigh. 'Beginning to feel more like the real victim now, *cara*?' He could not seem to stop the taunts from coming. 'It is a strange feeling, don't you think—being kind of frustratingly helpless? If we then start to wonder how our present lovers are going to feel when the news hits the stands, the sense of frustration really begins to bite.'

'You have a lover?' Her chin shot up, her slender neck twisting to show him blue eyes stark with horror and the glittering evidence of held-in tears. His inner senses shifted, stirring awake from what had only been a very light slumber anyway.

'Do you?' he fed back.

'Of course not!' she snapped. 'Do you really

think I would have got involved in any of this if I had a lover who could be embarrassed by it?'

'Whereas I was not allowed to make that choice,' he pointed out. 'So stop feeling sorry for yourself,' he finished coolly. 'You are still less the victim here than I am, so—'

'And you are just *so* loving being able to keep saying that to me!' Rachel got to her feet, restless, tense without knowing why.

Then she did know and she turned on him. 'So who is she—?' she speared at him as if she had the right to ask such a question.

Which she didn't, as the mocking glint in his eyes told her.

But it did not stop her stupid brain from conjuring up some other leggy blonde creature with a very expensive pedigree draping herself over him while he lounged in much the same way he was now—all long limbs and tight muscles and rampant sex appeal waiting to be adored because it was his due.

She took in a short breath, despising the heat of jealousy she could feel burning in her chest, as if a few angry kisses and a sham announcement had given her exclusive rights of possession over him!

It did not, but nor did it stop her crazy imagination from imprinting her own image of him. Her heart began pounding out a suffocating rhythm. This time she couldn't even look away! And to make it so much worse, having been crushed against him more times than was decent, she could even smell his sexy scent in her nostrils, feel the warmth of his mouth and the possessive touch of his hands on her—

'There is no one—fortunately…'

His deep voice slunk into her brain but she had to blink to make herself hear the words he'd spoken—then blink again to make herself understand what they meant.

He meant that there was no other lover in his life right now. Her mouth fell dry and her legs went hollow.

'I was just curious as to whether you had a man hanging about in the wings of this charade, ready to jump out and cause me more trouble.'

'Well, there isn't,' she confirmed and spun away, hating to hear him make that sardonic denunciation of her character because she knew he had every right to suspect her of every underhand trick there was going.

'Good,' he said. 'So I can sit here and enjoy

looking at my newly betrothed's fabulous legs without worrying if I am encroaching on someone else's territory.'

The aforementioned legs tingled. She moved tensely. 'We are not betrothed—'

'And the way the neat shape of her *derrière* is teasing me as it moves inside that tight little dress...'

Rachel swung round. 'Is this your idea of having fun, just to get your own back on me?'

'With compliments?' he quizzed innocently.

'Those are not compliments!'

'You don't like me to tell you that I like what I see—?'

'No—!' she lashed out.

'But it's okay for you to look me over as if you cannot believe your good fortune, is it?'

Rachel froze as a guilty blush ran right up her body and into her face. 'I w-was not—'

'Are your breasts your own?' he cut in on her insolently.

Her mouth dropped open in complete disbelief that he had actually voiced that question. 'How dare you ask me that?' she seethed.

'Easily,' he replied cynically. 'They look real, but who can tell by just looking these days—'

'They are real!' she choked out. 'And I've had enough of this—'

'No, you haven't.'

With only that small hint that something was coming, he sat forward and snaked an arm around her waist, then tumbled her down on to his lap.

Her cry of alarm doubled as a shimmering gasp when she found herself contained inside all of that long-limbed, hard-muscled strength.

'W-what do you think you're doing?' Her clenched fists pushed at his shoulders.

The gleam in his eyes mocked her. 'The way you keep looking at me, count yourself lucky that I lasted as long as I did.'

Oh, God, she'd been that obvious? 'You said y-you wouldn't do this—!'

'You are no longer helpless.'

He caught hold of her chin and pushed it upwards, his eyes hiding beneath half-lowered eyelashes as he waited for her lips to part with her next cry of protest—then he pounced, dipping his dark head to match the full pink quivering shape of her mouth with his.

So they'd kissed in anger. They'd kissed in a terrifying state of untrammelled lust. They'd kissed to shock and to subdue. But this—this was different. This contained so much hungry, frustrated, heated desire that it stirred her up more turbulently than any kiss she'd experienced in her entire life.

He explored her mouth so deeply that the feeling of being taken over completely drained her of the will to fight. Her clenched fists stopped pushing and opened to begin stroking in tight, tense, restless movements that only stopped when she found the warmly scented skin at his nape.

One of his arms held her clamped against him, the other stroked the length of her silk-covered thigh. Her dress had rucked up and the higher his hand glided the more she had to brace her inner thighs to try to contain what was happening there. And her breasts were tight, the nipples two stinging pinpricks pressing against the solid wall of his chest through his shirt.

Her fingers became restless again, one set moving to his satin cheekbone, then down in a delicate tremor to the corners of their straining mouths. He muttered something as he caught hold of her fingers and fed them down between them, until she was covering the hard ridge of aroused flesh pushing at his trousers. Frenzy arrived, a hot feverish frenzy of mutual desire that had been bubbling beneath the surface ever since their first kiss. Now it quickly spiralled out of control.

He caught hold of her hair and pulled her head back, his mouth deserting hers to wreak a trail of hot kisses down the arching stretch of her throat.

She was writhing with excitement, her skin alive to every brush of his lips and flickering lick of his tongue. A simple tug and the strap holding up her dress slipped off her shoulder. As clear air hit the thrust of her breast his mouth was continuing its delicious torment across its swollen quivering slope until he claimed the nipple with a luxurious suck.

An explosion of pleasure swept down from her nipple to low in her body, making her shudder, making her scythe out hot breaths as she clung to him.

Then his mouth came back to hers again and his tongue stung deep. Her deserted nipple was pulsating in protest at the loss of his exquisite suckling. She groaned into his mouth. He responded by lifting her up and bringing her back down straddling him without breaking the deep hot-mouthed kiss. She felt the thickness of his erection and couldn't stop herself from pressing into it. He encouraged her by clasping the tight mounds of her behind, now fully exposed because her dress was bunched to her waist. Flaming heat ignited between her thighs and she rocked her lower body, her fingers clutching at his silk-black hair.

When he stood up with her she didn't bother to protest. She knew what he was doing and where he was taking her. How he made it there without staggering she didn't know because his breathing was shot and his mouth had still not given up possession of hers.

The bed felt soft beneath her as he laid her down on it and she clung to his neck in case he decided to straighten and leave her, but he did no such thing.

Her dress was shimmied down her body. He stripped it from her legs with the deftness of a man who knew the easiest way to undress a woman without interrupting what was already happening with their mouths. There was no bra to remove—this dress was not the kind that permitted the wearing of one—and her stockings held themselves up, which left only her panties as a flimsy barrier to her complete nudity, but they stayed in place because he was now busy with his shirt.

She wanted to help; it was a feverish need that sent her fingers frantic as they tugged at shirt buttons, while his slipped lower to deal with his trouser-clasp and zip…

An impatient rustle of clothing, the fevered hiss of their breath, the heated scents from their bodies and the urgent touch of their fingers on newly exposed eager flesh…

And that deep drugging kiss just did not stop throughout all of it, not as she explored his muscle-packed contours or throughout each quivering gasp she made of pleasure when he explored her softer rounded flesh.

The impatient tug he gave at his shoes to remove them coincided with the reckless way that she dragged off his shirt.

Hot, taut satin skin adorned her hungry fingers once again, coated with a layer of male body hair. She scraped through it with her fingernails and felt him shudder with pleasure, her skin livening with excitement when she finally felt the full power of his naked length come to settle alongside her own. He was big and hot and amazingly, beautifully, magnificently built. Greedy for more, she rolled tight in against him and he accommodated her with a shift of his body that brought her into full contact with every part of his front.

The pouting buds of her breasts rubbed against the rough hair on his chest and she couldn't breathe for the tingling, stinging pleasure of it, yet she was panting, could barely cope with the thrills of excitement that went racing through her as he ran his hands down her spine and over her bottom and thighs to locate her stocking tops. He sent them sliding away with no effort at all. Her toes curled as the silk finally left them and he closed his fingers over her foot and used it to bend her leg over his hips.

Shock stung her into a quivering mass of pleasure when he captured one of her hands and fed it down to the velvet-smooth thickness of his penis, then urged her to stroke it between her legs.

He was big, a beautiful long-limbed muscular male with proportional length to his sex. She still had on her panties but she did not want them on; she wanted to feel him stroking like this against her with no barrier to dull the sensual ache.

Maybe he read her mind because he rolled on to his back, taking her with him, so she lay over him. Then he lifted her up and pushed her thighs together and ran his fingers into the scrappy fabric of her panties to stroke it away from the firm shape of her behind.

'Your skin is like silk,' he breathed against her urgent mouth.

When she caught the words with the flickering tip of her tongue he ran a forefinger into the tightly clenched crevice he'd uncovered and followed it all the way to the hot welcoming wetness between her legs.

He knew exactly what he was doing. Rachel just went wild as the dizzying tumult of thick, warm stimulation coiled around her senses. She moved with him in natural enticement and on a lusty growl he toppled her on to her back, then came to lie across her, their kiss completely broken for the first time.

His eyes were two intense black diamond orbs that he took from the burning desire suffusing her face to look down where his fingers now moved on her, following the path of pale dusky curls into soft female folds between her pearly-white thighs. The damp tip of his tongue appeared between his teeth as his dark head followed. For the next few minutes Rachel existed purely in the drugging eddy of his touch.

She was exquisite. The most receptive woman

he had ever experienced. There was a brief moment when he let himself wonder what man had taught her to respond like this. Then, as something too close to jealousy ripped at him, he thrust the question away. His fingers made a slow sensual journey to search out her pleasure spots, allowing his thumb to replace his tongue in rolling possession of her taut little nub. He looked back at her face and watched her sink deeper into helpless response, urged on by his burning need to drive her out of her mind.

Her pale hair lay spread out across his pillow, her parted mouth warm and full and softly gasping, her lips dewy-red against the whiteness of her wonderful skin. Her eyes were closed, her slender arms thrown above her head in complete abandon and the two peaks of her breasts swayed and quivered as she moved her body in a natural sensual rhythm with his caress.

And his heart was thundering against his ribcage, the ache of his own steadily growing need pulsing its demand along his fully aroused length. She wanted to come. He could feel the anxious ripple of her inner muscles bringing her swiftly towards her peak. But thinking about another man making her feel this good made him determined to heighten her pleasure some more.

So he ruthlessly withdrew and, as she whimpered out a protest, he stripped her panties fully away. Without pausing, he then began a long slow, tormenting assault with his hands and his lips and his tongue over every inch of her smooth pale flesh. Dipping his fingers yet again into her hot sweet centre, he closed his mouth round one of her breasts. They were so perfect, two plump pearly-white mounds of womanly softness, with pink super-sensitive tips protruding from their rose-circled peaks. His fingers toyed with one while his tongue toyed with the other. She groaned and arched and gasped and quivered and tried to pay him back with the hungry nip of her teeth. Her hands were everywhere on him now, exploring and stroking, sometimes sending him into paroxysms of shudders when she decided to score her nails into his flesh.

By the time he covered her, she was nothing more than a shimmer of sensation and he took her face between his fingers, then urged, 'Look at me,' in a dark husky voice that made her tremble as she lifted her heavy eyelids and showed him dark blue passion-drugged eyes.

He was so very beautiful, she thought hazily. A dark passionate lover with the face of a fallen angel. Rachel held his gaze as he eased himself between her slender thighs and made that first slow silken thrust inside, surprise widening her eyes as she felt his girth and length. She was no virgin, but he was big so maybe experience had taught him caution with a new lover because she could see his fight not to give her all of him gripping the perfect mould of his face.

'Okay?' he asked huskily.

She nodded, her tongue making a circle of her lips as she willed her inner muscles to relax. With an erotic slowness that fanned the flames flickering between them, he followed her circling tongue with his own. Her fingers were clutching at the bunched muscles in his shoulders, her breathing reduced to short gasps of air as he pushed deeper still. She could feel the roughness of his thighs pressing along the length of her silkier thighs and the way his lean buttocks clenched as the first sense-shattering ripple of her muscles played along his length.

It was a slow, slow merging like she'd never experienced—a careful all-consuming invasion that sent her mind spinning off somewhere and her senses taking on a singing bright will of their own. She moved restlessly beneath him, wanting all of him—needing all of him—but where her hands clutched his shoulders she could feel their bulging taut muscles were trembling with stress as he held himself back. Impatiently she lifted her hips, closed her eyes, then let her muscles draw him in deep.

Nothing had ever felt like this, Raffaelle thought on a lusty groan as the full pressure of his hips sent her thighs spreading wider apart and she took him into that hot tight tunnel with a gripping greed which sent shots of sensation rippling down his full length.

He claimed her mouth with a devouring kiss and she kissed him back so desperately that he flung caution aside and allowed the powerful flow to take him over. Half expecting protest, he received eager encouragement instead as the tactile muscle play of her pleasure surrounded him in moist muscle-livened heat.

She was amazing, a pearly-white sylph with the moves of a siren. Her arms were wrapped around his shoulders, her fingernails scoring deep into his flesh. He moved with increasingly harder strokes and she moved with him, taking each driving plunge from his flanks with an exquisite contraction which rewarded each exquisite thrust.

Energizing heat poured into both of them, driving the whole thing right out there into a different world. The real excess began to build like an electrifying life-force that fine-tuned itself between agony and ecstasy, liquidising the senses and shutting down the brain. The white heat of her orgasm took her over, lifting her whole body from the bed in a quivering arch and holding it there while he thrust and shuddered and ground out hoarse words as she pulsed all around him and brought him to a shattering climax that carried them on and on.

CHAPTER FIVE

AFTERWARDS they lay in a tangle of slack limbs, racing hearts and heated flesh. His face was pressed into the pillow next to her head as he fought for breath and Rachel lay pale as death with her eyes closed, trying desperately to block out the wildly wanton way she had just behaved.

Hot sex with a stranger. Her insides turned over.

She had never done anything like this before in her life.

Which did not make her feel any better about any of it.

Nothing, she suspected, was ever going to make her feel good about it. This was Raffaelle Villani spread heavy on top of her. The man with a notorious reputation for getting off with long-legged blondes.

Now she knew what it felt like to be just one of a large crowd. Self-contempt engulfed her, followed quickly by hot suffocating shame.

Maybe she moved or maybe she even groaned. She didn't think she'd done anything but he suddenly shifted, levering up his torso so he could withdraw that all-powerful proof of his prowess from inside her, and the worst shame of all came when she was unable to still her damning quivering response.

At least the way he shuddered told her that he was experiencing the same thing.

Pushing up on to his forearms, he lifted his dark head off the pillow and looked at her. One of those thick silences seized the next few seconds while Rachel tried hard not to burst into tears. Her heart was still pounding, the desire to duck and hide away almost impossible to fight. It didn't help that his expression was so sensuously slumberous, like a man who was feeling very—very satisfied.

'I...'

It was the only word Rachel managed to drag free from the tension in her throat.

'You—what?' he prompted huskily, reaching up with a long, warm, gentle finger to run it along the trembling fullness of her pulsing lower lip.

'I th-think we got carried away...' She breathed the words out over his finger because he had not lifted it out of the way.

'Well, you carried me away,' he said with an odd half smile that did not seem to know whether to be cynical or just rueful about the whole thing. 'You were—special.'

'Th-thank you,' she mumbled unhappily.

'Quite an unexpected…gift to come out of this mess tonight, which makes me so glad I did not turn away from it when I had the chance…'

A gift—he saw her as a *gift*?

Cynical, Rachel named his half smile, and tensed as the warmth still sandwiched between their two bodies began to chill.

'Well, turn away now, Mr Villani,' she responded frozenly. 'Because it's the last *gift* you are going to get from me!'

She gave a push at his wide shoulders and obligingly he rolled away to lie on his side, watching as she scrambled off the bed, then began hunting the littered floor for something to wear to cover up her nakedness. Catching sight of her dress lying there on the floor in a brazen swirl, she shuddered, hating the sight of it, and made a wild grab for his shirt instead.

'You sound very certain about that.'

'I am.' Rachel had to fight with the shirt sleeves, which had become tangled inside out.

'We were really great together…'

'Well, you're such a great lover,' she flicked back. 'Better than most, if that gives your ego a boost.'

'*Grazie.*'

Get lost! she wanted to scream at him. A gift—a *gift*!

The shirt slithered over her now shivering body and she dragged the two sides together with fingers clutching at the fine cloth like tense claws.

Flushed, angry, and aware that any second now she was going to explode on a flood of wild, uncontrollable I-*hate*-myself! tears, 'Is there another bedroom I can use?' she asked, chin up, blue eyes refusing to do anything other than look directly at his smooth, sardonic, lazily curious face because she was determined to get away with at least some small part of pride intact.

'You don't need one. This bed is easily big enough for the two of us.' He was supremely content in his languid pose.

Refusing to get into an argument with him, Rachel turned to walk towards the bedroom door.

'I don't do one-night stands,' he fed gently after her.

She stopped, narrow shoulders tautening inside

his oversized shirt. 'Neither do I...' she felt constrained to reply.

'Good. So we understand each other.'

'No.' Rachel swung round. '*I* don't understand!'

He was already off the bed and reaching for his trousers, so casual about his nakedness that she had to fight not to blush. He was incredible to look at: all golden and glossed by hard muscle tone, made all the more blatantly masculine by the triangle of black curls that swirled between his burgeoning pectorals and then drew a line down his torso to the other thick cluster curling around the potent force of his sex.

The stupid blush broke free when she recalled what that part of him had felt like erect and inside her. She tried to damp it all back down again but it was already too late because, as he was about to thrust a shockingly muscled brown leg into his trousers, he glanced at her and went as still as the dead.

Her breathing went haywire, her old friend panic rising up from places she did not know it could rise up from—her tender breasts, her taut nipples stinging against the cloth of his shirt and that terrible hot spot still pulsing between her legs, which made her draw in her muscles in an effort to switch it off.

He dropped the trousers. And she knew why he had. Seeing the way she was looking at him had turned him on like the floodgates opening on a mighty dam. What she'd thought potent before was suddenly downright unbelievable. He started walking towards her and she actually whimpered as she put out a trembling hand in the useless hope of holding him back, while her other hand maintained a death grip on the shirt to keep it shut across her front.

'No, please don't.' Her little plea came out all husky. Already her legs were threatening to collapse. 'We-we've made this situation messy enough as it is without adding intimacy to it—*please*!' she cried out when he just did not stop.

'I have just come inside you with the most amazing pleasure I have ever experienced,' his dark voice rasped over her. '*Intimacy* is here, *mia bella*. It is too late to switch it off.'

But it wasn't—*it wasn't*! 'I don't want—'

'Oh, you want,' he refuted. 'It has been vibrating out of you from the first moment we met. And I would be a liar if I did not admit to feeling the same way about you—so quit the denial.'

'Sex for the hell of it?' Rachel sliced back wildly.

'Why not?' Capturing her warding hand, he

used it to draw her in close. 'We are stuck with each other for the next few months while this thing plays itself out, so why not enjoy what we do have going here which is not part of the lie?'

'If I walk out of here dressed like this and tell anyone waiting out there that I changed my mind because you just were not good enough—that should finish it,' she suggested wildly.

'Are you telling me that my finesse is in need of practice?' He threw back his head and laughed. 'Since we both know that you seem to be pretty much a natural sensualist, Miss Carmichael, I give you leave to teach me all you know.'

'What is that supposed to imply?' Rachel stared up at him.

He grimaced and she didn't like the cynical gleam that arrived back on his face. 'Either someone taught you how to give a man unbeliev- able pleasure or it just comes naturally to you,' he enlightened. 'I was attempting to give you the more honourable benefit of the doubt.'

He was daring to suggest that she'd been trained like a concubine to pleasure men—?

First a gift, now a trained whore. Rachel stiff- ened like a board. 'How dare you?' she breathed furiously.

'Very indignant,' he commended. 'But I have just had the life essence squeezed out of me by the kind of muscles I did not know a woman could possess and you kiss like a delightful, greedy, well-seasoned Circe, *amore*—dangerous, but I'm hooked.'

'I think this has gone far enough.' She went to twist away from him.

He spun her back, broke her grip on the shirt front and ran his two hands inside it in a sensual act of possession that claimed her slender waist. Two long thumbs stroked the flatness of her lower stomach and her flesh turned into a simmering sensory mass. When she released an agonised breath he watched the way her pale hips swayed towards him as if they could not stop from hunting out closer contact with the burgeoning jut of his sex.

'Look at you,' he murmured. 'You cannot help yourself. That deliciously damp cluster of curls I can see crowning your thighs is crying out to feel me there again.'

'No,' she denied, knowing it was horribly, shamefully true.

'If I do this…' he eased her in closer and gently speared a path between her thighs '…your slender thighs cling to me as if your life depends upon it…'

And she was clinging. Weak and helpless. He rocked his hips and her arms just lifted, then fell heavily around his neck as she gave herself up to the pure pleasure of it. Her head tilted back, her blue eyes dark and her soft mouth parting and begging for his kiss.

He did not hold it back. He ravished her mouth while other parts of him ravished the soft folds of warm damp flesh between her legs. It did not occur to her that he was as much a slave to what they were generating between them. To Rachel he was just displaying his contempt for her. Toying with her because the humiliation of being made such an easy victim of her half-sister's messy marriage still stung his ego and he wanted her to pay for making him feel like that.

This was payback—sexual payback. And he meant to make her keep on paying for as long as this thing took to pan out.

She was picked up and tumbled back on to the duvet. He came to lean over her, blocking out the light like a domineering shadow, everything about him so physically superior, strong, mesmerising—overwhelming yet so potently exciting at the same time.

His eyes glinted down at her, his face a map of

hard angles built on arrogant sexual claim. She was about to be ravished a second time and the horror of it was that she knew she was not going to say no.

A telephone started ringing with the shrillness of a klaxon. Staring up into his face, tense and not breathing, Rachel thought for several seconds that he was going to ignore the call and continue with what he had started here.

Then his face altered, shutting down desire with the single blink of those long eyelashes, and he took hold of his shirt and grimly closed it across her breasts.

With that he levered himself off the bed, leaving Rachel to sit up and huddle inside the shirt while he went to recover his trousers and this time pulled them on.

He glanced back at her, nothing lover-like about him anywhere now. 'Get in the bed. Go to sleep,' he instructed.

Then he strode out of the bedroom, closing the door behind him, leaving Rachel coldly aware that she had just been put in her place.

As the *gift* in his bed, to use if or when he so desired it.

The telephone went silent. Unable to stop

herself, Rachel got up and went to open the door as quietly as she could, meaning to creep down the hall and listen in on the conversation—just in case it had something to do with them.

She did not need to take another step from where she was. The door on the opposite side of the hall was open. He was standing in front of a desk with his back towards her and his trousers resting low on his hips.

'You think that ringing me at two in the morning will please me, Daniella—?' His tone did not sound pleased at all.

Rachel continued to hover, watching as his naked shoulders racked up tighter the more that his stepsister said.

'Daniella…' he sighed out eventually. 'Will you give me the opportunity to speak? I am sorry you have been hit by so many telephone calls,' he said wearily. 'No, the lady in question is not Elise,' he denied. 'She is who she has always been. It is everyone else who made the mistake.'

A lie. Another lie. Rachel felt the weight of every single one of them land upon her shoulders.

Raffaelle turned sharply, as if he could sense her standing here. She watched his eyes move in a possessive flow from her face to his shirt, then down her legs. The intimacy in the look conflicted with the coldness now in charge of his features. And she knew that not only had he brought himself under control, but she was now looking at the man she'd first met, undeniably attractive but cynical and hard.

On a wavering grimace Rachel dropped her eyes from him and stepped back into the bedroom. When Elise had picked him to have her rebellious affair with, she had chosen the wrong man, she thought heavily as she closed the door.

Pushing his free hand into his trouser pocket, Raffaelle suppressed the desire to either curse or sigh as he leant his lean hips against the edge of the desk while Daniella continued to yell in his ear.

He was angry with the interfering press, who were taking it in turns to call up Daniella in their quest for more information. He was also fed up because the whole thing was now driving itself like a train with no damn brakes.

And he was achingly bloody aroused and despising himself for feeling like that. Where did he get off, jumping all over a woman—a *stranger*—like some randy, feckless, uncontrolled youth—?

No wonder she'd looked at him just now as if

he had crawled out from beneath a stone. No wonder she had gone back in the bedroom and shut herself away. She knew she was trapped; *he* knew he was trapped!

'No, Daniella,' he grimly cut in to her half-hysterical ranting. 'It is *you* who made the mistake two months ago. She was *never* Elise—have you got that?'

His cold tone alone had the desired effect.

'You mean you want me to *say* that I was mistaken?'

'No. I am telling you that you *are* mistaken.'

'So you *have* just got engaged to marry this Rachel Carmichael—the same woman who threw herself at you tonight?'

'*Si,*' he confirmed.

'Just like that—?' She was almost choking on her disbelief.

'No, not just like that,' he sighed out. 'I have been—courting Rachel over the last few months.'

'*Courting* her—?'

Bad choice of word. '*Seducing* her, then.'

Her struck silence made him grimace and he couldn't make up his mind if she was beginning to swallow the lies or simply being sensible for once and taking on board the grim warning in his voice.

'Is she pregnant—?'

'No!' he bit out, jerking upright from the desk and swinging round as a sting of stark alarm shot down his back.

Dio, he'd used nothing to stop it from happening, and he had not thought to ask her if she was protected!

What kind of crass bloody oversexed fool did that make him? Or her for not thinking about it—?

'And, since my personal life is no one's business but my own, *cara,* can I suggest a simple *no comment* from you would make me happy? Or, better still, Daniella—take the telephone off the hook!'

He cut the connection and tossed the handset back on its rest, then just stood there, not knowing what to do next.

Sex without protection with a woman he barely knew. Flexing muscles rippled all over him as he took on board the consequences which could result from such a stupidly irresponsible act.

With his luck tonight, she could already be in the process of conceiving his baby. Add all the other risks which came along with unprotected sex and he suddenly felt like a time bomb set to go off!

A growl left his throat as he turned back to the

bedroom. Chin set like a vice, he pushed open the door. The room was in darkness. He switched on the overhead light and went to stand at the bottom of the bed.

She was nothing but a curled up mound beneath the duvet. 'I did not use protection,' he clipped out.

The mound jerked, then went still for a gut-clenching second. Then it moved again and she emerged, sliding up against the pillows, flush-cheeked—wary, defensive—sensationally delectable.

Dio, he thought.

'Say that again,' she shook out.

'I did not use protection,' he repeated tautly. 'I am not promiscuous and I have never taken such risks before in my life,' he added stiffly. 'I like to think that I can respect my…partner's history in the same way that she can respect mine.'

Rachel looked at the way he was standing there like some arrogant autocrat caught with his pants down by his bitch of a wife. Only his pants were up; it was his shirt that was missing and the bitch of a wife in this case was the *gift* he'd been handed and enjoyed thoroughly—before he'd thought to wonder where she had been before she'd landed in his bed!

As if it wasn't bad enough that she was sitting in the bed belonging to a man she had only met for the first time tonight, wearing his shirt and his scents and his touch on her skin—she now had to endure the kind of conversation that belonged in a brothel!

Next he would be asking how much he owed her for her services. Give him half a chance and she knew he would love to denounce her out loud as a whore.

Well, what did that make him? Rachel wanted to know.

'I am a clean-living, careful, healthy person,' she snapped out indignantly.

'I am relieved to hear it.'

He didn't look it. 'I don't sleep around! And if you hit me with one more rotten insult, Mr Villani,' she warned furiously. 'I think I am going to physically attack you!'

'My apologies if it sounded as if I was trying to insult you—'

'You did insult me.' She went to slide back down the bed.

'But we don't know each other.'

'You can say that again,' Rachel muttered.

'And it is an issue we need to address.'

'Well, you addressed it very eloquently,' she told him and tugged up the duvet with a *now go away* kind of shrug.

If he read it he ignored it. 'We have not finished with this.'

'Yes, we have.'

'No, Rachel, we have not…'

It was the alteration in his voice from stiff to weary that forced her to take notice. 'We still have the issue of another kind of protection to discuss.'

Another kind… Rachel froze for a second, then slid back up the pillows again, only this time more slowly as she finally began to catch on.

He put it in simple words for her. 'I did not protect us against—conception. I need to know if you did.'

It was like being hit with one hard knock too many; she felt all the colour drain from her face. 'I don't believe this is happening to me,' she whispered.

Taut muscles stretched as he pulled himself in like a man trying to field his own hard knock. 'I presume from your response that it is a problem.'

'I've told you once—I don't sleep around!' she cried out.

A nerve flicked at the corner of his hard

mouth. 'You don't need to sleep around to take oral contraception.'

'Well, thank you for that reassuring piece of information,' she said hotly. 'But, in my case, and because *I don't sleep around*, I—don't take oral contraception either...' The heat in her voice trailed into a stifled choke.

He cursed.

Rachel covered her face with her hands.

She had just indulged in uninhibited sex with a stranger without any protection; now his millions of sperm were chasing through her body in a race towards their ultimate goal!

Fertilisation. A baby—dear God...

Suddenly she was diving out of the bed and heading at a run for the bathroom. She thought she was going to be sick but then found that she couldn't. She wanted to wash herself clean inside and out!

Instead she just stood there with her arms wrapped around her middle and shook.

She heard him arrive in the door opening. 'I h-hate you,' she whispered. 'I wish I'd never heard your stupid name.'

Raffaelle shifted his tense stance, relaxing it wearily so he was leaning against the doorframe.

He wanted to echo her sentiments but he did not think she was up to hearing him say it while she stood there resembling a skittish pale ghost.

'It happened, *cara*. Too late now to trade insults,' he murmured flatly instead.

She swung round to stare at him, blue eyes bright with anger and the close threat of tears. 'You think that kind of remark helps the situation?'

Pushing his hands into his trouser pockets, Raffaelle raised a black silk eyebrow. 'You think that your previous remark helped it?'

No, she supposed that it didn't.

Losing the will to stand upright any longer she sank down on to the closed toilet seat. 'I'm so horrified by what we've done.'

'I can see that.'

'I don't w-want a baby,' she whispered starkly.

'Any man's or just mine?'

Rachel looked at the way he was standing there in the doorway—*lounging* there half-undressed. A tall, lean, tightly muscled *supremo*, the image of everything you would want to grab from the human male gene pool.

Feeling something disturbingly elemental shift in her womb, she went on the attack. 'Being flippant about it doesn't help.'

'Neither does flaying yourself.'

She stared at him. 'Where the heck are you actually coming from?' she gasped out. 'You don't know me, yet you stand there looking as if you couldn't care less about what we've done!'

'I am a fatalist.'

'Lucky you,' Rachael muttered, pushing her hair back from her brow. 'Whereas I am wishing that yesterday never began.'

'Too late to wish on rainbows, *cara*.'

'Now you are just annoying.'

'I apologise,' he drawled. 'However, since we could well be in this for the long haul, I suggest you get used to my—annoying ways.'

'Long haul—?' Her chin shot up. What was he talking about now?

'Marriage comes before babies in my family,' he enlightened.

Marriage—? 'Oh, for goodness' sake.' It made her feel sick to her stomach to say it, but— 'I'll take one of those m-morning after pills that—'

'No, you will not,' he cut in.

She stood up. 'That is not your decision.'

His silver eyes speared her. 'So you are happy to see off a fragile life before it has been given the chance to exist?'

'God, no.' She even shuddered. 'But I think it would be—'

'Well, don't think,' he said coldly. 'We will not add to our sins if you please. This is our fault not the fault, of the innocent child which may result. Therefore we will deal with it the honourable way—if or when it comes to it.'

'With marriage,' she mocked.

'You must know I am considered to be quite a good catch, *cara*.'

Softly said, smooth as silk. A sharp silence followed while Rachel took on board what he was actually implying. Then she heaved in a taut breath. 'I suppose I should have expected that one,' she said as she breathed out again.

'I don't follow.' He frowned.

'The—you set me up for this accusation.' She spelled it out for him. 'The—you got me into bed deliberately so you could position yourself as the great millionaire catch!'

'I did not say that.' He sighed impatiently.

Oh, yes, he damn did! Inside she was quivering. Inside she was feeling as if she'd stepped into an ice cold alien place.

'I'll take the other option,' she retaliated and went to push past him. The hand snaking out of his pocket grabbed her by the arm as the other hand arrived, holding a mobile telephone.

'Let go of me.'

He ignored her and there was nothing relaxed about him now, Rachel saw as he hit quick-dial, then put the phone to his ear.

'Are we still under siege from the press?' he demanded.

He had to be talking to the security man in the foyer, Rachel realised. A new kind of tension sizzled all around them while he listened to the answer and she waited to find out where he was going with this.

The hard line of his mouth gave a twist as he cut the connection. Sliding the phone back into his pocket, he speared her with a hard look.

'The paparazzi is still out there,' he stated grimly. 'I do not expect them to leave us alone any time in the near future—understand?'

Rachel just stared at him, all eyes and weighty heart and pummelled feelings.

'Wherever you or I go from now on, I can almost guarantee that they mean to follow.' He made his point brutally clear. 'So think about it, *cara*,' he urged grimly. 'Do you want to take a walk out to the local all-night pharmacy and turn this thing into a tabloid sensation as the pack follow to witness you purchasing your morning-after medication—?'

Ice froze the silence between them as diamond eyes locked challengingly with frosted blue. Rachel thought about screaming. She felt like screaming! He really, truly and honestly believed that she was ruthless enough to calmly take something to rectify the wrong they had done, his wonderful *fatalist* attitude giving him the right to believe that his morals were superior to her own.

And why not? she asked herself starkly. What did he really know about her as a living, breathing person? Hadn't she flipped out the clever counter attack to his marriage deal? Wasn't she the cool liar and cheat around here, who could hit on a man and let him take her to his bed for no other reason than she'd fancied him?

Why not tag her as a woman who was also capable of seeing off a baby before she was even sure that there was one?

Hurt trammelled through her body, though, melting the ice and turning it into tears because she could not deny him the right to see her as a cold, ruthless schemer—she'd painted her own portrait for him to look at, after all.

He saw the tears and frowned. 'Rachel—' he murmured huskily.

She pushed his hand off her arm and walked away, only to pull to a hovering halt in the middle of the bedroom.

Nowhere to run. Nowhere to hide, she realised as her tears grew and grew. In the end she did the only thing she could see open to her right now and climbed back into the bed and disappeared beneath the duvet again.

Heart thumping, eyes burning, she pressed a clenched fist against her mouth to stop the choking sobs she could feel working their way up from her throat.

She heard him move. The lights went off. A door closed quietly. He had the grace to leave her alone with her misery and at last she let the first sob escape—only to jerk and twist her head on the pillow just in time to see him lift up the duvet and the warm dark shape of his now fully naked body slide into the bed.

Her quivering gasp was lost in the arm he used to draw her against him. Eyes like diamonds wrapped in rich black velvet searched her face, then a grimace touched his mouth.

'You're crying,' he said huskily.

'No, I'm not.' Squeezing a hand up between them, she went to brush a stray tear from the corner of her eye.

Or she would have done if one of his fingers had not got there before hers took the tear away; she could not hold back another small sniff.

'I would not have done it,' she mumbled.

'*Si*, I know that.' He sighed. 'We were fighting. You used your weapon well. I retaliated by cutting you to pieces. I apologise for doing it.'

'You're so ruthless it's scary.'

'*Si*.' On another sigh he sent one of his legs looping over her legs to draw her in a bit closer to him, then he caught her hand and pressed it to his chest.

She felt his warmth and his muscled firmness and the prickle of hair against her palm. It was all very intimate and very dangerous—especially so when she didn't try to pull away. The shirt formed a sort of barrier to stop the more frightening skin to skin contact, but—

She eased out a sigh of her own and tried to ignore what was happening to her. 'I'm really sorry I got us both embroiled in this mess,' she whispered in genuine regret.

'But you did do it,' he pointed out with devastating simplicity. 'Now we have to deal with what we have.' He came to lean over her, suddenly deadly serious. 'And what we have is one story, one betrothal, one bed,' he listed. 'You will not, during the time we are together, give cause for anyone to question our honesty.'

'Our lies, you mean.'

He shook his dark head. 'Start believing in this, *cara*,' he advised. 'The fate of your sister's marriage rests on your ability to live, breathe and *sleep* the role you have chosen to play in my life.'

His life. Those two words said it all to Rachel. This was *his* life he was protecting. His reputation. His pride.

And why not—? she thought painfully. Her mouth quivered. The tip of his tongue arrived to taste her soft upper lip.

Rachel saw that grimness had been replaced with slumberous desire and knew what was going to happen next.

'No,' she jerked out.

But his tongue dipped deeper. 'Yes,' he contradicted in soft silken English.

'But I don't—'

'You do, *cara*,' and he showed her how much she did by trailing his fingers inside the shirt.

Her breast received his touch with livewire tingles. Don't respond! she told herself, but she did. Her mouth opened wider to turn the gentle contact into a proper kiss and the globe of her breast peaked pleasurably against his palm. It was terrible; she could not seem to control herself.

On a husky murmur he took the kiss back from her and from there it all began to build again.

It should have been a huge let-down after what they'd just been fighting about—but it wasn't. What it was, was a slow, slow attack on every sensual front he could discover by using his lips and his tongue and the light-light tantalising brush of fingers. There was not a single millimetre of her flesh that was not gently coaxed into yielding its secrets—its every weakness exposed and explored until she felt like a slave to her own sensuality and an even bigger slave to his.

By the time he prepared to come into her, she was so lost in a hazy world made up entirely of him that she just lay there, watching while he produced the protection they'd both forgotten about the last time and expertly rolled it down his powerful length.

His eyes burned hers as he came over her. When he pushed inside, her groan brought his lips down to capture the sound. They moved together in a slow, deep, serious, dark journey, which left both of them totally wiped out by its end.

And, as sleep finally swept her into boneless oblivion, Rachel knew she had been totally taken over, ravished, possessed.

I wish, was the last conscious thought she remembered having and fell asleep wondering what it was she had been about to wish for.

She awoke cocooned in a nest of warm duvet and to the sound of a telephone ringing again. Only it did not sound loud, as if it was being muffled by the thickness of walls and doors. But the persistent sound pierced through her sleep like a sluggish pulse taking place inside her head.

She didn't open her eyes—didn't want to. Too many bad memories were already rushing back, the worst of them being the knowledge that she'd fallen into bed with a man she'd only met the night before, had hot, unprotected sex with him and now his physical imprint was so deeply stamped on her that she could still see him, hear him, feel him and smell him with every sensory cell she had.

The ringing stopped. Rachel let her eyes open. Daylight was shrouded by the drawn curtains but she could see just enough to know that the place beside her in the bed was empty and she breathed a sigh of relief.

At least she would have some time to get herself back together before she had to face him again.

Easing out of the bed, she rose to stand up with just about every muscle feeling the extra stretch as she looked around her for something to put on.

Her clothes had gone. So had the shirt she had been coveting last night like a last line of defence. What now? she asked herself. Were her missing clothes supposed to be sending her a message about where she fitted into his life?

Suddenly spying the cashmere throw he had used to cover her with the night before draped over a chair, she leapt on it and wrapped herself in it. The throw covered her from throat to ankle but she still felt like the wretched man's concubine, imprisoned for his exclusive use.

And he knew how to use her, she was forced to admit when her senses gave a tight little flutter in response to the thought.

Someone knocked on the door. She almost tripped over as she spun round to stare at it.

'Y-Yes?' she called out, puzzled as to why the

heck he was bothering to knock when privacy had been something he had taken no heed of last night.

'Your things have arrived, Miss Carmichael,' a totally strange female voice announced. 'Shall I leave the suitcase here outside the door?'

'Oh—y-yes—thank you,' she answered, frowning because she didn't know what the woman was talking about.

She waited a few seconds before going to pull the door open a small crack to make sure the woman had gone before she looked down to discover the suitcase she'd hastily packed before leaving Devon was now standing on the floor. Clinging to the black throw with one hand and still frowning, she used her other hand to lift the case inside the bedroom and shut the door again.

Last time she'd seen this, it had been lying open and spilling its contents on to the spare bed in Mark's flat. So how had it ended up here instead?

Had Mark delivered it? Had he come here, then left again without bothering to see or speak to her to find out if she was okay?

Hurt thickened her throat as she heaved the case on to the rumpled bed and unzipped it. Inside it was everything she had brought up to London with her, plus all the extras that Elise had provided to help turn her into her look-alike.

There was also a piece of paper lying on the top of everything. Picking it up, she unfolded it to find it was a hastily scribbled note from Mark.

Did you have to send the chauffeur round to knock me up for your stuff at 6 o'clock in the morning? I'd only just crawled into bed!

Elise called you last night after I told her the good news, but your phone was dead. She and Leo wanted to congratulate you on your coming nuptials, if you get my drift. Call her later today so she can play the ecstatic sister for Leo's benefit.

I'm off to LA this afternoon for a few weeks. See you when I get back. Love M.

Mission accomplished, in other words, so it was back to normal life—for Mark anyway. No words of concern for how she was feeling. No sign of a rescue plan for her any time soon.

Rachel stared out at nothing for a moment or two. Then, as a rueful grimace played its rather wobbly way across her mouth, she let the note fall on to the bed and turned her attention to selecting fresh clothes from the suitcase. At least she was now overloaded with expensive hair products and cosmetics, she consoled herself.

Dressed in a short bathrobe and fresh from his shower in one of the guest rooms, Raffaelle opened the bedroom door as the bathroom door shut with a quiet click.

He stood for a moment, viewing the evidence of her occupation, then walked over to the bed and picked up the note. His expression hardened as he read it. His eyes then drifted to the open suitcase, where it looked as if everything had been dumped in there at haste.

Did she feel deserted? She had to feel deserted because it was exactly what had happened to her.

Replacing the note where he'd found it, he turned then and strode across the bedroom to open the door which led into his dressing room. Ten minutes later he was dressed and letting himself out of the bedroom as quietly as he had come in while the running shower still sounded from the other side of the closed bathroom door.

CHAPTER SIX

IT TOOK nerve for Rachel to open the bedroom door and step into the hallway. She would rather be doing anything than facing Raffaelle Villani in the cold, harsh light of day.

Rubbing her hands up and down her arms in a nervous gesture as she walked, at least she looked more like herself, she tried to console herself. With Elise's image stripped away and her hair shampooed and quickly blow-dried, she'd seen the real Rachel staring back at her from the mirror—the one who wore jeans and a long-sleeved black knit top. Her make-up was minimal and her hair had reverted to its natural style.

All she needed to do now was to convince herself that she was the real Rachel, because she certainly did not feel like her inside.

She intended to go and hunt down her bag and her cellphone before she did anything else, but she never got that far. The door next to the kitchen stood open and, having glanced through it, she then pulled to a heart-sinking halt.

Raffaelle was there, standing by a long dining table. He was wearing a soft loose-fitting smoked-grey T-shirt and a pair of charcoal trousers that hung easily around his hips. And, if she had ever wanted to know the difference between expensive man dressed in a formal dinner suit and expensive man dressed casually, then she was looking at him.

The aroma of fresh coffee would have sailed right by her if he had not used that moment to lift a cup to his mouth. She was held transfixed by his height again, by his sensual dark good looks, by his mouth sipping coffee and his long golden fingers holding the cup.

Sensation quivered right down her front as each and every sense unfurled and responded to the sight of those hands, that mouth, the long legs and wide shoulders—to her exciting new lover. Her breasts grew tight and tender in her bra cups, her tongue grew moist in her mouth, her breathing stopped completely as a tight tingling erupted low down. It was like falling into a deep, dark pit of forbidden pleasures. She didn't want to feel like this but she could not break free from it.

Then he glanced up and caught her standing

there staring at him. It was like being pinned to a wall by her guilty thoughts. Heat rushed up from her toes and through her body until it suffused her face to her hair roots while he just stood there with his cup suspended just below his sensual mouth.

The agony of mutual intimacy was nothing short of torture as she watched his eyes drop to the pair of simple flat black shoes adorning her feet, then begin a slow journey upwards, along well-faded denim that clung to her legs and her hips and the flatness of her stomach like a second skin.

His scrutiny paused right there and suddenly something else was adding to the turbulent mix. Rachel knew what he was thinking. She felt the muscles around her womb clench tightly as if it was acknowledging that it already belonged to him.

Maybe he saw the tightening because his eyes darkened. When he lifted them to clash with her eyes, the sheer power of what was passing between them put her into a prickling hot sweat.

He broke eye contact and she could feel her heart drumming against her ribs as he dropped his attention to her mouth, slightly parted and trembling, with its light coating of pink lipstick, then back to her eyes, looking out at him from a fixed hectic blue stare between quick flicks of mascara.

Finally he let his eyes drift over her hair, where long and sleek straight had been replaced by a mop of silky loose curls that framed her still blushing face.

'Where did the curls come from?' he asked softly.

Forced into speech, Rachel had to moisten the inner surface of her lips. 'They were always there, just hiding,' she answered, lifting a self-conscious hand up to push the curls from her brow.

He continued to stare as the curls bounced back into place again. Shoulder-length straight now finished in a sexy blonde bubbly riot almost level with her pointed chin.

'They suit you,' he murmured.

'No, they don't,' she denied. 'But I was born with them, so...' She added a shrug, then stuck her hands into her jeans pockets and finally managed to drag her eyes away from him.

Raffaelle frowned as he watched the defensive body language.

'Is there any of that coffee going spare?' she asked.

'Sure,' he answered. 'In the kitchen. I will go and get it—'

'No.' She jerked into movement. 'Let me.'

She'd disappeared before he could stop her,

fleeing like a scared fluffy blonde rabbit. It made him grimace—a lot of things made him grimace, like the tension she'd taken with her—the knowledge of what they'd done the night before. And the lack of awareness in her own natural beauty, for which he placed the blame firmly at her glamorous half-sister's feet.

Draining his coffee cup, he made the decision to follow her. Now the morning ice was almost broken he had no intention of letting it freeze over again.

She was standing by the coffee machine, watching it fill a cup.

'Here,' he said, striding over to offer his empty cup. 'I like it black.' He moved away from her before she had a chance to react to him. 'What do you like for breakfast—a fresh croissant? Cereal? Toast?' he listed lightly. 'There is some fresh orange juice in the fridge if you—'

'I don't want anything,' she cut in. 'Th-thank you,' she added. 'Just a caffeine shot then I will have to be going…'

'Going…' He turned slowly to look at her.

'Yes,' She was clearly refusing to look at him, staring down at her watch instead. 'I have a train to catch back to Devon and half the morning has gone already.'

'We've been over this,' Raffaelle reminded her. 'You are staying right here with me.'

'Yes, I know that.' She nodded, setting the blonde curls bouncing as she concentrated on the job of swapping her filled cup for his empty one beneath the stream of coffee from the machine. 'But I need to get some clothes if...'

'I will buy you any clothes you will need.'

Rachel stiffened. 'No, you will not! I have clothes back in Devon—and don't you *dare* make such a derisory offer like that again!'

'It was not derisory,' he denied. 'I was being practical.'

'Well, I'm trying to be practical too, and I can't just drop everything as if I don't have another life. I need a couple of days to—organise things with the farm.'

'You mean you actually run the farm yourself?'

More derision? Rachel stared at him but only saw honest disbelief in his face. 'Efficiently,' she stated coolly.

'So who is looking after it while you are here?'

'A—neighbour.' She frowned as she said that, wondering why she had put her relationship with Jack in such odd terms. 'But he has his own place to run, so I...'

Something altered in his demeanour, though Rachel wasn't sure exactly what it was.

'Use your phone to make your arrangements, as I have had to do,' he said coolly.

'God, you're so insufferable,' she gasped. 'It's all right for you. You're Mr High-flyer. You can order people about by phone, but I can't.'

Ignoring the high-flyer quip, Raffaelle walked towards her. 'You think?'

'I know.' Rachel nodded backing into the corner of the kitchen units as he approached, then feeling well and truly trapped by the time he towered over her. 'I've seen the way it works with Leo. W-when he needs something done he just throws his weight around by telephone.'

'But you need to be hands-on to water your organic lettuce,' he mocked.

'You don't need to be so derisive about it!' she flashed in her own defence. 'When this is all over with, Mr Villani, you might be unfortunate enough to have lost a deal or two because you weren't paying proper attention, but I risk losing my whole livelihood!'

'If you are carrying my child then this will never be over.'

Placed coolly into the argument, Rachel swallowed thickly. 'Don't start hitting me with the worst thing that could happen again,' she shook out huskily.

He went to say something, then sighed and changed his mind. Tension stung—antagonism that wasn't all to do with what they were arguing about.

'You said it was family-run thing,' he then prompted.

'It is,' she confirmed. Then she took a breath and altered that answer to, 'It *was* a family run thing until my parents were killed five years ago in—in a road accident. Now the farm is split three ways between me, Mark and Elise.'

'Which means that you do the work and they do nothing?'

'I like the work, they don't.'

'Loyal little thing, aren't you?' he mocked her. 'Has it not occurred to you yet that they are not very loyal to you—?'

Raffaelle wished the words back as soon as he'd said them. But it was too late. She'd already gone pale and she lost her cup so she could make a defensive fold of her arms across her front.

'My family loyalty is none of your business,' she muttered.

'You think—?' Anger with himself made his

voice sound harsh. But since the anger was there now, he took a grip on her clenched left hand and prised it upwards. 'This ring on your finger demands that I should have your complete loyalty now.'

'It's fake.' She grabbed the hand back and thrust it beneath her arm again.

Things were starting to happen. Fights with women usually did end up as sexual battles and Raffaelle was beginning to feel the sexual pull. He reacted to it by snaking his hands around her slender nape and tilting her head back so he could claim her mouth.

She tasted of mint toothpaste and pink lipstick. He found he liked the combination. And she didn't try to fight him, which he liked even more. By the time he raised his head again, her arms were no longer defensively crossed but clinging to his shirt.

'This isn't fake,' he rumbled out deeply, still toying with the corner of her mouth. 'So let's forget about Devon and go back to bed. I don't know why we got out of it in the first place.'

'No.' She gave a push at him and when he released her she scuttled sideways. 'I've got things to do.'

'You mean you're running scared all of a sudden.' He grabbed her hand to pull her out of the kitchen and back into the dining room. 'If you are hoping to escape to a pharmacy in Devon,' he said brusquely, 'then first you should take a look at these…'

He brought her to a stop beside the dining table where a selection of the Sunday tabloids lay spread out.

Rachel froze, wondering how she had missed seeing them before. But she knew why she'd missed them; she'd been too busy drinking him in to notice anything else in the room.

In every photograph but one, she and he were standing outside the apartment block displaying the ring and looking convincingly loverlike and besotted. The only photograph that was different was in Mark's paper, which bore the clever caption, *'First public kiss for newly engaged lovers.'*

'My fifteen minutes of fame,' she jibed tensely, looking at the sleek stranger in the photographs, who happened to be her. Raffaelle looked no different than his tall, dark, handsome self and how he'd managed to pull off that smile without making it look cynical was worthy of a headline all by itself.

'This is set to last a lot longer than fifteen minutes, *cara*,' he responded dryly.

'Because you're newsworthy.'

'Which is the only reason why you hit on me in the first place,' he pointed out. 'This is what you wanted.' He waved a long finger at the photograph her half-brother had taken. 'I must admit you look very like your sister in that.'

The picture showed a clinch which looked like they'd been lovers for ever. That wave of tingling intimacy shot down Rachel's front again and she quickly shifted her eyes to the other more carefully staged photographs, all of which were accompanied by catchy tag lines aimed to turn them into tacky celebrity fodder.

'I did not want all the rest of this, though. That was your fault.'

'You cannot be so blind.'

It was the way he said it that made Rachel look sharply at him. It had been hard and sardonic—tones that repeated themselves in the expression on his face.

'Explain that,' she demanded.

'I meant nothing.' He went to turn away.

'Yes, you did!' She caught hold of his arm. 'And I want to know what you meant!'

He swung back to her, face hard, eyes angry. 'Did you never think to question if your brother's cronies would know who his twin is? Of course they knew—' he answered his own question '—which is why they came after us and called out Elise's name. They saw you looking like her and him making his quick escape, then they saw a very contrived yet really juicy scandal brewing involving Elise, Leo Savakis and Raffaelle Villani in a gripping sex triangle. I can forgive you your naïvety, *cara*, if you are as shocked as you appear to be, but I will not forgive your stupid brother for not thinking this thing through and foreseeing the obvious outcome if I had not intervened!'

Rachel pulled out a chair and sat down on it. He was oh-so-sickeningly right. And the worst of it was that he seemed to have worked all of it out within seconds of her explaining it all last night.

'Now ask yourself how long you think it will take the press to sleuth out exactly who you are,' he persisted. 'And your fifteen minutes of fame becomes a roller coaster ride to hell and back while they dig into your past, with Leo Savakis waiting in the wings for you to fall off the rails and accidentally reveal it is all just a big ugly cover-up for his wife's transgressions.'

'You don't have to say any more,' Rachel whispered. 'I get the full picture.'

'Do you?' he rasped. 'Well, add this into the mix. Start running scared now and I will blow the whole lie sky high and damn your sister's marriage. I can take the heat of the repercussions if she cannot!'

He walked out of the room, leaving Rachel alone to stew on what he'd said. It didn't take long. He was right and she had been running scared when she'd made that bid to leave here and go back to Devon. But that had nothing to do with the lies, though they were bad enough. Her reasons did not even have anything to do with their stupid delving into unprotected sex!

It was to do with him and what he did to her. What he made her feel. If he could affect her this badly in only one night, then she was going to be an emotional wreck by the time it came to the end.

If it came to an end, she then amended, recalling that marriage warning he'd made.

Raffaelle was pacing his study wondering what was the matter with him. Why had he bitten her head off like that?

Because she wanted to go home to collect some clothes and organise her life, or because she still persisted in defending her selfish family?

Or was it because she'd mentioned a man down there in Devon? A *neighbour* she had not bothered to mention before…?

He did not know. He did not think he *wanted* to know. Something was happening here that scared him witless each time he came close to looking at it.

He heard her moving about then and went to see what she was doing now. He found her in the living room with her bag in her hand.

'I—can't find my phone,' she said and she looked pale and defensive again.

'The battery was flat. I put it on the charger in my study. I'll go and get it…' Then he paused. 'Who do you want to call?'

Irritation ripped down his backbone because he knew it was none of his business who she wanted to call. By the expression on her face, she thought the same thing.

Still, she answered him. 'I will have to ring round a few people if I am not allowed to leave here—'

'No.' Raffaelle shook his head. 'We will do it your way, only we both go and we will use my car instead of the train.'

'But—'

'Ten minutes,' he said gruffly, turning away

again. 'And don't keep me waiting. The sooner we leave, the sooner we can get back.'

He drove them in a silver Ferrari with the same reckless efficiency he'd driven the night before. But then, his driving had had to be nifty when they'd met with the paparazzi waiting outside for them to leave. They'd picked the car up from the basement car park but the moment they'd emerged on to the street they'd been spotted and all hell had broken loose as camera-toting reporters fell over themselves to get into their cars and give chase.

'I don't understand why they're still hanging around,' Rachel said after they'd lost their pursuers in a sequence of dizzying turns down narrow back streets. She hadn't dared speak before then in case she broke his concentration and they ended up hitting a wall. 'What do they think we are going to do? Get married on the apartment steps or something?'

'They don't know enough about you.' He sounded so grim that Rachel felt a cold little shiver chase down her spine.

'I hate this,' she whispered. 'I hated it when I used to get caught up in it with Elise. I don't know how you people live your lives like this.'

'We live in a celebrity-driven world,' he answered levelly. 'The masses are greedy for the intimate details of the rich and famous—or, for that matter, anyone who lives a high profile life. You have now joined the celebrity ranks, so get used to it, because this is only the beginning of it.'

The beginning of it...

After that Rachel did not speak another word. They reached the motorway and suddenly the powerful car came into its own, eating up the miles with the luxurious smoothness that promised to cut the journey time by half.

He stopped once at a motorway service station, led her into the café and bought sandwiches and coffee.

'Eat,' he instructed, when she stared at the unappetizing-looking sandwich he'd placed in front of her. 'You look like death and you have eaten nothing since you threw yourself at me last night.'

And I look like death because I hardly had any sleep last night, she threw back at him without saying the words out loud. Because out loud meant opening a Pandora's box full of what they'd been doing instead of sleeping.

The indifferent-tasting sandwich was washed

down by indifferent-tasting coffee. Rachel was surprised he ate his sandwich or drank the coffee. They just didn't look like the kind of food this man would usually put anywhere near his mouth.

When they hit the road again he wanted to talk. 'Tell me how your family works,' he invited.

So she explained how her mother had lost her husband to a long-term illness while the twins had still been very young. 'A few years later she married my father and then had me.'

'So what is the age difference between you and the twins?'

'Six years,' she replied.

'And who did the farm originally belong to?'

'My father. But he—*we*—never differentiated between Mark and Elise and myself. And it isn't really a farm,' she then added because she thought she better had do before they arrived there and he saw it. 'It's what we call a smallholding, with three acres of land, a house, a couple of greenhouses and a couple of barns.'

'Another lie, *cara*?'

Rachel shrugged. 'It's run like a farm.'

'And the…neighbour that helps you out when you need it—what does he do?'

'Jack owns the land adjoining our land—and

his *is* a farm,' she stressed. 'He's been good to us since our parents died.'

'Call it as it is,' Raffaelle said. 'He has been good to *you*.'

Rachel turned to look at him. 'Why that tone?' she demanded.

His grimace stopped her from becoming hooked on watching his face. 'I don't think I want to elaborate,' he confessed.

'Suits me,' she said and, turning the collar up on her coat, she leant further into the seat and closed her eyes.

His low laugh played along her nerve endings. 'You are prickly, Miss Carmichael.'

'And you are loathsome, *Signor*.'

'Because I don't mind saying that I dislike the way your siblings use you?'

'No. You are loathsome simply because you are.'

'In bed?'

Rachel didn't answer.

'You prefer, perhaps, this Jack in bed as your lover because he is so *good* to you.'

He was fishing. Rachel decided to let him. 'Maybe.' She smiled.

'But can he make you fall apart with pleasure there as I can, or does he bring the smell of farmer to your bed, which you must overcome before he can overcome you?'

'As I said. You're loathsome.'

'*Si,*' he agreed. 'However, when I said that I don't sleep around I meant it, whereas you seemingly did not.'

Rachel turned her head and flicked her eyes open to look at him. Once a liar always a liar, she thought heavily when she saw the grimness lashed to his lean profile.

And a tease could only be a tease when the recipient knew he was being teased. Sitting further up the seat with a sigh, she pushed a hand through her curls and opened her mouth to tell him exactly who and what Jack was—when her attention was caught by a giant blue motorway sign.

'Oh, heck,' she gasped. 'We need to take this next turn-off!'

With a startled flash of his eyes and a few muttered curses, he flipped the car across several motorway lanes with one eye on the rear-view mirror judging the pace of the traffic behind them and the other eye judging the spare stretch road in front of them. By the time they sailed safely down the slip road Jack's name had been washed right out of Rachel's head by an intoxicating mix of nerve-fraying terror for her life and the exhilarating thrill of the whole smooth, slick power-driven manoeuvre.

'Which way?' he demanded.

Rachel blinked and told him in a tense breath-stifled voice while her senses fizzed and popped in places they shouldn't. What was it about men and danger that struck directly at the female sexual psyche?

He glanced at her and saw her expression and sent her a wide slashing masculine grin that lit her up inside like a flaming torch.

'Scared, *cara*?' he quizzed.

'You—you—'

'Had it all under control,' he smoothly provided. 'Which, in Italian terms, makes the difference between a mere good lover and a fabulous lover.'

Rachel knew exactly what he meant, which was the hardest thing to take. If he stopped the car now she would be crawling all over him in a hot and seething sexually needy flood.

It was everything—the powerful car and the reckless man and the adrenalin rush still singing through her blood. She tried to breathe slowly and lost it completely when he reached across to her and gently stroked her cheek. Static fire whipped across her skin cells, she whispered something and turned her head. Their eyes clashed. For a short, short split second in time it was like falling into a vat of writhing, hissing, snapping snakes.

He looked away. The smile had gone but the atmosphere inside the car had heightened beyond anything real. Rachel sat on her hands to stop them reaching for him and tried to pretend it wasn't happening while he drove on with a sudden grim concentration that only made everything worse.

She gave directions in short, sharp, breathless little bursts of speech that only helped to increase the tension. He said nothing but just reacted with slick control of the car. They were both sitting forward in their seats. They were both staring fixedly directly ahead. She knew where this was going to end up just as he knew it. And the agony of knowing was as tough as the agony of having to sit here and wait.

At last—finally they turned into the private lane which led to the farm. Winter fields barely waking up to early spring spread out on either side of them, neatly ploughed and ready to sow. The old farmhouse stood in front of them, its

MICHELLE REID   165

rustic brick walls warmed by a weak sun. Flanking either side of it stood the adjoining barns and behind the house they could just see the greenhouse's glass glinting in the weak sunlight.

In front was the cobbled yard where Rachel's muddy old Jeep stood tucked in against a barn wall. On the other side stood another car, a Range Rover, making Rachel's heart sink, though whether that was due to disappointment, because she knew what was buzzing between the two of them was about to be indefinitely postponed, or relief for the same reason, she refused to examine.

Raffaelle brought the car to a stop in the dead centre of the courtyard, killed the engine, then climbed out without uttering a word. Rachel was slower in moving, unsure if her stinging legs would hold her up if she tried to stand on them.

He couldn't know what was coming and she didn't know how to tell him. One glance at his face across the top of the car and she was almost bowled over by the strict control he was holding over himself.

His eyes were not under control, though. They looked back at her with a possessive glitter that showered her with sexual promise.

She parted her paper-dry lips. 'Raffaelle—' she began anxiously.

'Let's go inside and find a bed,' he said huskily.

She quivered and swallowed, then heaved in a tense breath in preparation to speak again. The front door to the house suddenly swung inwards, snatching her attention away from him.

He looked where she was looking, shoes scraping on worn cobbles as he turned then went perfectly still.

A man stood in the open doorway—a tall, well-built, swarthy-looking man wearing brown cords and a fleece coat. He was also a man easily in his fifth decade, with eyes like ice that he pinned on Raffaelle.

'Jack,' Rachel murmured, feeling trouble brewing even before she saw Raffaelle tense up when she said Jack's name.

Damn, why hadn't she thought about this before she'd teased Raffaelle about her relationship to Jack?

And, oh dear, but Jack did not look pleased at all.

She hurried forward. Raffaelle stood frozen as he watched her walk straight into the other man's arms. He was trying to decide whether to go over there and punch the bastard for taking advantage of a vulnerable young woman left alone here to cope on her own. Or to reclaim what now belonged to him, then tell him to get the hell out.

In the end it was the other man who took the initiative.

'Jack…' Rachel burst into nervous speech as she reached him. 'This is…'

'I read the paper this morning, Rachel,' he cut in, looking across the cobbles with a set of grey eyes that were as cold as Raffaelle's own eyes.

He put her to one side so he could walk forwards. Rachel could feel the suspicion coming off him in waves. Jack knew her better than most people, so if anyone was going to smell a rat about her surprise engagement then it would be him.

'I n-need to explain.' She dashed after him.

'Mr Villani,' Jack greeted coolly.

Nerves jumping all over her now, Rachel rushed into speech yet again. 'Raffaelle, this is Jack Fellows.' Her anxious blue eyes pleaded with him to understand. 'He's my—'

'Guardian,' Jack himself put in. 'Until she is twenty-five, that is.'

'Well, that is a new name for it,' Raffaelle drawled.

'Jack is also my uncle,' she said heavily. 'M-my mother's brother…'

'And the one who looks out for her interests,' Jack coldly put in. 'So, if you are the same Italian who broke Rachel's heart last year, then you had better come up with a good reason for doing it or Rachel will not receive my blessing for this engagement.'

Oh, dear God. Rachel wished the ground would open up and swallow her. It just had not occurred to her that Jack would make such a mistake!

Now Raffaelle was looking at her as if she was one of the devil's children and she couldn't blame him. It had to feel as if each time he turned around he was being forced to answer new charges that someone in her family planted at his feet!

'Raffaelle is not Alonso,' she muttered to Jack in a driven undertone.

'Was that his name?' Her uncle looked at her in surprise. 'I don't recall you actually ever mentioning it.'

That was because she hadn't. She'd just come back here from her trip to Italy looking and behaving like a woman with a broken heart.

Her uncle turned back to Raffaelle. 'My sincere apologies for the mistake, Mr Villani,' he said and offered him his hand.

But it was too late for Rachel as far as Raffaelle was concerned. She sensed his anger hiding beneath the surface of his smile as he took Jack's proffered hand.

Then he switched the charm on. By the time he had finished explaining who he was and what he was, and trawled out the same story about how and where he'd met Rachel, he had her uncle eating out of his hand. It was like watching an action reply of the way he had handled the press the night before. And all Rachel could do was smile benignly once more and be impressed by his performance, while knowing retribution was close at hand.

He coolly assured Jack that he was no fortune hunter out to marry his niece for her share in the family pile. He assured him dryly that no, not all Italian men were so cavalier with the vulnerable female heart.

And of course he was madly in love with Rachel—what man would not be? His arm snaked out to hook her around her shoulders so he could draw her in close to his side.

I'm going to kill you the minute I get you alone, that heavy arm promised. And Rachel believed it—totally.

Then he apologised to Jack that the news of their betrothal had broken in the papers before he'd had a chance to come here and officially request Jack's blessing.

It was his finest moment, Rachel acknowledged from her subservient place at his side. Jack was old-fashioned, with traditional values. She could see from her uncle's expression that in Raffaelle he thought he was meeting a man after his own heart.

Jack had to rush off then but he offered them dinner to celebrate.

Smooth as silk, Raffaelle thanked him but regrettably had to decline. Apparently he had to be back in London this evening—to attend an irritating business dinner.

Whether there was a business dinner, Rachel did not know. But, of course, her uncle understood. Busy men and all that.

And Raffaelle's ultimate coup was to gain Jack's instant agreement that everything here would be taken care of while Rachel was away, because of course Raffaelle wanted her with him.

'Just be happy, darling,' Jack said to her, then he kissed her cheek, shook Raffaelle by the hand and left them, driving away while they stood and watched him—with Raffaelle's arm still exhibiting its possession across her shoulders in a grip like a vice.

Happy was the last thing she was feeling by the time her uncle's car disappeared out of sight. The moment he turned them to face the house Rachel tried to break free from him but his grip only tightened as he walked them across the cobbles.

The front door opened directly into the farmhouse-style kitchen, heated by the old Aga against the wall. Coming in here should have felt comfortingly familiar to Rachel but it didn't. The door closed. The arm dropped from her shoulders. Moving like a skittish kitten, she took a few steps away from him then spun around.

'I...'

'If you are about to utter yet another lie to me—' he cut right across her '—then let me advise you to keep silent!'

CHAPTER SEVEN

HER heart gave a thick little thump against her ribcage. It was like looking at a complete stranger again—a tall, dark, coldly angry stranger.

'I was actually about to apologise for the…misunderstanding with Jack out there.'

'You set me up.'

'It w-wasn't like that,' she denied. 'Y-you were fishing for information and I stupidly decided to tease you about my relationship with Jack.'

'I am not referring to your desire to pull my strings by intimating there was another man in your life,' he said. 'Though using your uncle like that is unforgivable enough.'

'Then what—?' she demanded.

'Alonso,' he supplied. 'The Italian heartbreaker I have been set up to play substitute for in your desire for payback!'

'That's not true!' Rachel protested.

His angry eyes crashed into her like a pair of ice picks. 'Not only is it true but you are the most devious witch it has ever been my misfortune to come into contact with!' he incised. 'This was never just about saving your half-sister's marriage! You always had this hidden agenda in which I paid for the sins you believe your other Italian lover committed!'

'No!' she cried. 'I'm *not* that petty! Elise's problems are serious enough without you adding such a crazy accusation into the mix! And anyway,' she said stiffly, 'you are nothing like Alonso. In fact I couldn't compare the two of you in any way if I tried!'

'In bed, perhaps?' he grimly suggested. 'Did you close your eyes and imagine it was him you were driving out of his head with your thrust-and-grind gyrations and those exquisite little muscle contractions?'

'No!' she said hotly. 'How dare you? That is such a rotten thing to say!'

'Then who did teach you to make love like that?' He took a step towards her. 'How many men, *amore,* does it take to produce such a well-practised sensualist?'

Blushing hotly, she cried, 'I'm not listening to this—'

She turned towards the door that led through to the rest of the house. The way he moved so fast to slam a hand against the door to keep it shut had her shivering out a shocked gasp.

'Answer the question.' He loomed over her.

Rachel folded her arms. 'You so love to throw your weight around, don't you?'

'Just answer.'

Anger flicked her eyes up to meet his. 'Why don't you tell me first—how many women have slipped in and out of your bed to make you such a *fabulous* lover?' she hit back. 'What was that,' she mocked when he clenched his expression. 'Do you want to tell me it's none of my business?'

'I am thirty-three years old, you are twenty-three.'

'Meaning the ten year difference justifies the numbers you clearly don't want to give?'

His shoulders shifted. 'I do not break hearts.'

Rachel released a thick laugh. 'You wouldn't know if you broke hearts! Men like you don't go into sexual relationships with the care of tender hearts in mind, *Signor*. They go into them for the sex!'

'In your experience.'

She tried to push past him, but the muscles in his arm bunched to form an iron bar she could not pass. 'Yes,' she hissed out.

'Gained mostly from this Alonso guy who took only what he wanted from you and trampled on the rest?'

'Yes!' she said again. 'Happy now?' she demanded. 'Have you got the required information nicely fixed in your head? I've had *two* lovers. Both Italian. *Both* with their brains lodged in their pants!'

For some reason she hit out at him, though she didn't understand why she had. The feeble blow barely glanced off his rock-solid bicep. And she was beginning to tremble now and didn't like it—beginning to bubble and fizz with anger and resentment and the most horrible feeling of all—humiliation at the way Alonso had treated her!

So maybe Raffaelle was right: when she'd agreed to hit on him to save Elise's marriage some subconscious part of her had wanted to pay back Alonso.

'So I am playing the fall guy.'

He was reading her thoughts. She swallowed tensely.

He turned to push his shoulders and head back

against the door. '*Dio*, I cannot believe I fell into this trap.'

Rachel struggled to believe that she had fallen into it all too. 'I vowed I would never go near another Italian.'

'*Grazie*,' he clipped. 'I wish you had kept to your vow.'

Rachel turned away and walked over to the Aga and put the kettle on to boil. Why she did it she hadn't a single clue because she knew she could not swallow even a sip of anything right now.

But at least the move put distance between them. Silence hummed behind her while she removed her coat and laid it over the back of a kitchen chair. Outside a weak sun was trying its best to filter into the room through the window on to scrubbed pine surfaces that had been here for as long as she could remember, yet she still felt as if she were standing in an alien place.

'Where did you meet him?'

The brusque question startled her into glancing at him. 'Who—?' she bit out.

His shoulders almost filled the doorway, his dark head almost level with the top of the frame. His face was still angry, the clenched jawline, the flat mouth, the glinting hard eyes, yet its harsher beauty still riveted her to the spot and claimed her breath and sent the hot stings of attraction streaking through her veins.

'My heartbreaking rival,' he provided and moved at last, shifting away from the door to pull out a chair at the table and sit down.

'In Italy.' Rachel moved to the sink and began toying with the mugs left there to drain. 'I was working on a farm just outside Naples—w-work experience,' she explained. 'He lived there. We met. Within a week I was moving into his apartment…' Wildly besotted with him and madly in love. 'He told me he loved me and, like a fool, I believed him. When it came time for me to come back to England, he said thanks for the great time and that was it.' She picked out two mugs at random. 'Do you want tea or coffee?'

'Coffee—when was this?'

'Last summer.' Shifting back to the Aga, she put the mugs down and picked up the coffee jar, then suddenly put it down again.

It had been only last summer when Alonso had taught her a lesson about Italian men she'd vowed never to forget. Yet here she was, involved with another and threatening to make the same mistakes all over again.

'I need to—do a few things before I can leave here. Can you make your own coffee—?'

She had disappeared through a door before Raffaelle could say anything—running scared again, he recognised as he sat there listening to her footsteps running up a set of stairs.

Then, on an angry growl, he got up and went to stand by the window. One part of him was telling him to go after her and insist she finish telling him the whole miserable story about her Italian lover—her *other* Italian lover, he grimly amended. Another part of him was wondering why he was not just climbing into his car, which he could see standing outside on the cobbles, and driving away from this…fiasco before the whole thing leapt up again and bit him even harder!

Because it *had* bitten him already, a voice in his head told him. She could already be carrying his child.

'*Dio*,' he breathed. He could not remember another time in his life when he had been so thoroughly stung by a woman.

And he did not need all of this hassle. He had many much more important things he could be doing with his time than standing here wondering what she was doing upstairs where he could hear her moving about just above his head.

Leo Savakis was not really his problem—none of this was his damn problem—except for the as-yet-unconfirmed child. He did not need to hang around until they discovered the result of their mindless love-in. A telephone call in a month would make more sense than hanging around her like this.

Yet some deep inner core at work inside him was stopping him from getting the hell out of here.

Lust, he wanted to call it. A hot sexual attraction for a devious female with cute curly blonde hair and the heart-shaped face of an innocent but who made love like the most seasoned siren alive.

He had taught her how to be that person—that other Italian lover had tutored her on how to give the best of pleasures to a man, had then dumped her as if that was all she had been good for—a student of his sexual expertise and a boost for his ego.

And then there was that thing with *real* teeth which was biting at him. He was used to being desired for himself. He was used to being the favoured one women revolved around, waiting with bated breath to find out which one of them he would choose.

Arrogant thinking? Conceited of him to know that he only had to crook a finger to have them crawling with gratitude around his shoes?

Yes. He freely admitted it. His clenched chin went up.

With Rachel Carmichael he was learning very quickly what it felt like to come in as second best in the heart and mind of a woman.

He did not like it. It gnawed at his pride and his sexual ego. And if he needed to find an excuse for why he was still standing here instead of driving away, then there it was.

There was no way that he was going to accept second best to any other man. By the time this thing between them was over, his Italian rival was destined to be nothing but a vague shadow in her distant memory.

She'd gone quiet.

Raffaelle looked up at the ceiling. What was she doing up there—lying on her bed pining for the heartbreaker?

Rachel was sitting on her bed with her cell-phone lying in her palm displaying a text message from Elise.

Thank you for doing this for me. I will love you always. Leo is over the moon about the

baby. He's taking us to Florida on a long overdue holiday. I could not be happier. He sends
you his congratulations! Tell R thanks for his
understanding. Have a great time playing the
rich man's future bride!

What a wonderful game, Rachel thought bitterly.
What a great way to waste several weeks of her life.

If she still had a rich future husband to play the
game with, that was. He could have come to his
senses and made his escape while she was up
here moping—driven away in a cloud of dust and
offended pride!

Getting up, she walked over to the window that
overlooked the courtyard. The silver Ferrari still
sat there glinting in the shallow sunlight. Relief
was the first emotion she experienced—for
Elise's sake, not her own, she quickly told
herself.

Then the bedroom door suddenly opened and
she turned to see him standing there, filling the
gap like he had filled the other door downstairs
and her senses responded, reaching down like
taunting fingers to touch all too excitable pleasure
points and she knew she was relieved he was still
here for no one else's sake but her own.

'*Ciao*,' he murmured huskily.

'*Ciao*,' she responded warily, searching his face for a sign that another battle was about to begin and feeling the taunting brush of those fingers again when she saw that anger had been replaced by lazy sensual warmth.

'Need any help?' he asked lightly.

'Doing what?' Rachel frowned.

'Packing.' Walking forward, his gaze flicked curiously around a room made up of countrified furniture complete with chintzy soft furnishings. 'I see no sign of it happening yet,' he observed. 'But then—' his eyes came back to hers '—maybe you have other ideas for how we can spend the rest of the afternoon—?'

It was like being tossed back into the pit of writhing snakes again.

Switch off the anger and let desire rush back in, she reasoned. 'I d-don't think—'

'Good idea—let's both not think.' He moved in closer. 'That small flowery bed looks the perfect place to spend a few hours thinking of nothing at all but this…'

But this—but this… His arms came around her and his mouth took over hers. No one needed to think about doing this, although—

'Why?' she whispered. 'Y-you should…'

'Be turned off you because you keep showing me different faces?'

His fingertips combed through the curls on her head as if to remind her of one of those changes she had made once already today and—damn her, but Rachel felt herself almost purring into his touch like a cat stroked by its beloved master.

He saw it and, on a soft laugh, caught her full, softly rounded, inviting mouth. It was one of those bewitching, tasty, compulsive kisses that clung, tongue tip to tongue tip. She swayed closer and his hands caught her waist to feel the slender arching of her spine for a few seconds before he gently but firmly drew her back.

'You get to me, Rachel, you really get to me. Though God knows why you do, because I certainly don't.'

'Not your usual type?' She could not resist the dig because while he frowned at her she was tingling in places that should not do that—the nerve-endings along the length of her inner thighs and between her legs.

He shook his head. 'Not my usual anything,' he muttered. 'You answer back, you disrespect, you lie and you cheat without batting an eye.'

'I don't cheat—!' she protested.

'Then what do you call the woman I first met last night with the long straight hair and the couture dress?'

A cheat. He was right.

'Well, this is the real me,' she said as she took a step back from him. 'The one with curls and jeans and—if you give me the chance—the one constantly fighting with dirt beneath her chipped fingernails…' She looked down at her nails, frowning now because they looked so different from what she was used to seeing: clean, well manicured and—pink. 'I am not made to be a *femme fatale*, Raffaelle. I wasn't even that good at it last night, only you didn't notice it because you were seeing what you'd been conditioned to expect to see at a function like that.'

'You were damn good at what came afterwards,' he said brusquely. 'I'll take a rain-check on the *femme fatale* bit if I can have more of that.'

Her chin went up, blue eyes coolly challenging. 'And the cheating face I'm supposed to show to the real world? Does it pop on and off according to what you require from me?'

To her surprise he let loose one of those lazy sexy smiles that melted the hardness out of his face. 'I think I like the idea of that. I will keep the sensual curly-haired Circe all to myself while the rest of the world gets the *femme fatale*.'

'Complete with fake ring to go with the fake relationship.' Rachel heaved out a sigh. 'We shouldn't be doing this at all.'

'Too late for regrets, *cara*. We have been over this already. We are both into this up to our necks.'

'Not the sex part.'

'Yes, the sex part!' he contended. 'It is here. We have it. And since it is the area where you really do get to me, we keep it.'

'If I say no?'

His laugh was derisive. 'You would have to want to say no and you don't.' He lowered his head to toy with her lips again. Electrifying, seducing. 'Do you—?' he challenged her for an honest answer.

Since her lips were clinging and her hands had already found their way beneath his T-shirt to the satin tight warmth of his skin she could not very well give any other answer than a weak shake of her head.

'Then say it so I can hear it.'

'I want you,' she whispered, swaying closer to him again, wanting, *needing*, body contact.

His hands on her waist held her back. 'Say my name,' he insisted.

Say his name... Alonso was suddenly looming up between them again. She tugged in a tense breath.

'I did not think of any other man but you last night, Raffaelle.' She felt she owed it to him to tell him that.

His murmur of satisfaction brought his mouth back to hers again with a full-on hot, deep, sensual attack. At last he was letting her have what she craved the most—skin-to-skin contact with him. Her fingernails curled into satin-tight flesh, then followed the muscular line of his ribcage across his chest, then around to his back so she could punish him at the same time as she arched even closer.

He shuddered, deserting her mouth. 'You ruthless witch,' he muttered as he took a moment to grip the edge of his T-shirt and rake it right off. Hers followed suit before he would allow her any more of his mouth.

Like that they strained against each other, exploring with their hands, tongues and lips. He was perfect. No man should possess a body like his. Rachel tasted his skin, her hands moving possessively over his hair roughened contours while he stood there and let her enjoy him, encouraging her with kisses and slow strokes of his hands.

Neither of them noticed that they were still standing in front of the window. Rachel with her back to it, Raffaelle with the sheen of the sinking sun painting his skin rich gold with a hot coral glow. He buried his fingers in her hair and pulled her head back to receive the full onslaught of his kiss.

Lights flashed, explosions took place. In the dizzying urgency of two lovers who needed to move this thing on to its next passionate stage, they missed that those explosive flashes came from outside the window.

The camera-toting paparazzo, who'd picked up their trail where others hadn't, slunk off down the driveway back to his car parked in the lane. He was smiling, pleased with himself, while the two captured lovers continued what they were doing, Rachel reaching up her arms to wind them round Raffaelle's neck as he lifted her up so her legs could cling to his hips. The bed was two steps away and he toppled her on to it, then bent to rid of her tight-fitting jeans.

He stood back. 'Tell me what you want,' he demanded as he began to strip.

'You,' she whispered.

'And who am I?'

'Raffaelle,' she sighed out—then sighed again as the full burgeoning thrust of him was arrogantly displayed.

He made her repeat his name throughout the long hours that followed. By the time they drove away from her home the intimacy between them had evolved into something beyond sex.

They arrived back at his apartment midevening. Raffaelle cooked them a meal while Rachel unpacked her clothes, grimacing at the array of sleek designer hand-me-downs Elise was forever giving to her, which most women would kill to own, but which she had rarely ever had an occasion to wear. Now they took up all of her hanging space in Raffaelle's dressing room as if they reflected the person she was now.

But she wasn't, was she?

They ate in the living room, lounging on a rug with their backs resting against one of the sofas and the television switched on. Rachel ate while she tried to concentrate on what was happening on the TV screen when really she was already hyped up about what was to follow.

Crazy, she told herself. You know none of this

is real. You must be mad to let him get to you this badly.

Then he reached out to pick up her wineglass from the low table in front of them and handed it to her and their eyes clashed. What was good or bad for her became lost in what happened next. He moved in to kiss her; she fell into the kiss. The glass went back to the table and they made love on the rug between bowls of half-eaten pasta with the television talking away to a lost audience. Afterwards he carried her, satiated and too weak to argue, to bed.

'The pots and things…' she mumbled sleepily.

'Shh,' he said. 'I will see to them,' and he left her there.

By the time Raffaelle came back into the bedroom she was asleep. When he slipped beneath the duvet he did not disturb her—he did not think he had the energy to cope with what was bound to ensue if he did.

He closed his eyes, wanting sleep to shut out the next few hours before he had to make any decisions about how they were going to tackle the rest of this. The great sex was one thing, but the realities of life still waited out there for him to deal with.

Lies built on more lies. Smothering the urge to sigh, he shifted his shoulders against the pillows. She moved beside him, turning in her sleep to curl in close to him, her soft breath warm on his neck and a cool hand settling lightly on his chest.

He looked down at it resting there, with its pale slender fingers and pearly-pink varnished nails, and his skin burned in response to what he knew it could make him feel.

Lies or not, she was in his blood now. A fantasy siren most men would kill to possess. He closed his eyes again and tried to hunt down that illusive thing called sleep. His last conscious thought was the grimly satisfying knowledge that she was almost worth the temporary loss of his freedom and the trail of subterfuge he was about to embark upon.

Unless Mother Nature decided to get in on the act.

He fell asleep on that thought.

The next day brought fresh problems to deal with. He had been drinking coffee in the kitchen and trying to put his head in order while Rachel still lay lost in sleep in his bed, when his housekeeper arrived and laid a tabloid down in front of him.

'I thought you might want to see this,' she murmured embarrassedly.

But one glance at the photograph was enough to send him into the bedroom. 'Rachel, wake up.'

He shook her gently, then watched as she did her trick of emerging from the duvet in that way which grabbed at his senses.

'We need to talk,' he said grimly, then dropped the paper on to her lap.

Silence hung for the next thirty seconds while he stood there waiting and she looked down at the newspaper. There was something disturbingly erotic about the way the photograph had caught them and he knew by the way she suddenly dropped her face into her hands that this was one intrusion too far.

A nerve at the corner of his hard mouth gave a twitch. 'I suppose that being caught on camera like this will kill the suspicions of any mocking doubters and prove that we are indeed what we appear to be. But from now on both of us must be aware of what we do and what we say even when we believe we have complete privacy.'

'Life in the fast lane,' she named it bitterly.

'*Si*,' he agreed. 'I am used to it—though not to the degree that I feel the need to hide behind closed curtains,' he put in cynically. 'I would have expected that, having a half-sister like Elise and an insight into your half-brother's way of earning his living, you would know all the pitfalls of life in the fast lane.'

At last Rachel lifted her head to look at him. 'Are you implying that I set this up too?' she demanded.

'No,' he denied. 'I am simply advising you to draw on your knowledge gained from both of your siblings and think carefully before you move or speak.'

'It sounded more like a command to me.'

'Call it what you want,' he said. 'But accept that you will not go out without someone with you,' he instructed. 'I will assign one of my own security people to escort you.'

It was only as he said it that Rachel realised she was stuck here in London, in his apartment with nothing to do. Elise was away. Even Mark was away. She didn't know anyone else in the city! While it was very obvious by the way he was dressed that he was not going to hang around here if at all possible and keep her company.

'So I'm to be a prisoner now as well as your…' She severed the rest but they both knew what she had been about to say.

'It cuts both ways, *cara*,' Raffaelle said unsympathetically. 'I had a life and relative freedom with which to live it until you threw yourself at me. Now I have you, a bed and no life to call my own.'

'At least you get to go to work.'

'It is what I do during the day.'

'Well, lucky you.' Rachel handed him back the newspaper, then she curled on her side and tugged the duvet up to her ears. 'I might as well stay right here then, since it's the only place I am useful.'

He laughed. 'Hold that delightful thought until I return.'

Then he was gone. The door closed. He strode down the hallway and out of the apartment, then into the lift. It took him down to the basement where Dino and his limo awaited him. The moment he settled in the rear seat and opened his laptop his business cellphone began ringing and real life settled in. As he concluded his fourth complicated call of the journey, Dino was pulling the car to a stop outside the Villani building. He climbed out and strode in through the doors into familiar surroundings where that other excitement which came a very close second to sex waited to take him over.

Then it came.

'Congratulations, Mr Villani!'

'Congratulations, sir!'

Congratulations resounded from every corner.

The curious smiles that accompanied them were due almost entirely to the photograph printed in this morning's paper, he judged.

His smile was mocking but fixed. And even that was wearing thin by the time he hit the top floor of the building.

'Congratulations, Raffaelle,' his secretary greeted him and dumped a whole load of telephone message slips down on his desk.

'What are those?' he asked dubiously.

'Congratulations and invitations, of course.' She grinned. 'I would hazard a guess that these are only the beginning. It looks as if you and Miss Carmichael will be dining out every night for months!'

He gave her them back. 'You deal with them.'

'Me?'

'Filter out the rubbish and sort the rest into some kind of order,' he instructed. 'Then I will look at them.'

'But wouldn't it be more appropriate if Miss Carmichael did it?'

Recalling the woman he had just walked away from brought a gleam to his eyes. 'No. She has better things to do,' he murmured dryly.

Like playing his personal little sex nymph.

CHAPTER EIGHT

THE SEX NYMPH WAS UP, showered and dressed in jeans and a T-shirt by the time Raffaelle entered his office building to a barrage of congratulations.

The sex nymph could not be more prim and polite when his housekeeper introduced herself as Rosa, the chauffeur's wife; apparently both of them travelled everywhere that Raffaelle went.

And the sex nymph had no intention of being anywhere near the bedroom by the time he got back home again.

She had come up with a much more practical way to spend her time.

Over a light breakfast prepared by Rosa, Rachel planned her day with the concentration of a tourist determined to miss nothing out. Only her tour would not consist of historical sites in the city; she was going to trawl the restaurants and food wholesalers specialising in organic produce.

Her nice new security guard arrived conveniently as she was about to leave. His name was Tony and he had the use of a car, which meant far less footwork.

Still, by the time she had been delivered safely back to the apartment long hours later, she was almost dead on her feet.

Raffaelle was crossing the hall towards his study from the living room as she stepped in through the door. Pinstriped jacket gone, shirt sleeves rolled up, tie knot hanging low at his throat and glass slotted between his fingers, he looked deliciously like the successful man just in from work and ready to wind down from his busy day.

Rachel paused, completely held by his sexual pull.

He paused too and looked at her, silky curls ruffled, face still chilled by the cold breeze blowing outside, woollen coat unbuttoned to reveal a white T-shirt with a neckline that scooped low at the front. He took his time taking in every detail with the slow—slow thoroughness of a seasoned connoisseur of beautiful women.

Knowing that she lacked the connoisseur's high standards right now sent Rachel's chin shooting up, blue eyes challenging him to say something derogatory.

'Did you enjoy your day, *mi amore*?' was the sarcastic comment that fell from his lips.

Defences heightened, she reluctantly supposed she should explain where she'd been. 'I went...'

'I know where you have been,' he cut in. 'Tony works for me, not for you.'

'Then, yes—' they could both play with polite sarcasm, she decided '—I had a very enjoyable day, thank you. And you?'

'I had an...interesting day,' he replied, watching her every step as she made herself walk forward. 'I spent it giving polite replies to polite invitations for us to dine with polite people who cannot wait to get a better look at my future wife.'

Recalling the revealing photograph in this morning's paper sent a rush of heat into her cool cheeks.

'Of course you did the wise thing and politely declined those polite invitations?'

'No, I accepted—most of them.'

Rachel pulled to a standstill. 'I hope you're just teasing.'

He took a sip of his drink, every inch of him vi-

brating with a kind of sardonic challenge that gave
her his answer before he shook his dark head.

'The show must go on.'

'But I don't want to meet your friends!' she
protested.

'Scared they might see through us?'

'Yes!' she said. 'Can't we just want to—be alone
together—as real engaged couples prefer to be?'

'You're mistaking a new betrothal with a new
marriage,' he countered. 'Honeymooners want
to—be alone together. Newly betrothed couples
want to get out there and—show off.'

'But I don't want to show off!'

A satin black eyebrow arched in enquiry. 'You
don't think I am good enough to show off?'

'Don't talk rubbish,' she snapped. What woman
in her right mind would say he wasn't fit to show
off? 'I just don't think *we* are fit to be seen as an
intimate couple within a group of your friends!'
Stuffing her hands into her coat pockets and
hunching her shoulders in self-defence, she went
on, 'I presumed we would do—safer things like
go out to quiet restaurants or something.'

'A restaurant it is.' He smiled. 'Eight o'clock.
We will be meeting my stepsister and several
other close friends of mine.'

Rachel's stomach started rolling sickly. 'Tonight?' she squeezed out painfully.

'*Si*,' he confirmed.

'W-why couldn't you be friendless?' she tossed out helplessly.

He just grinned. 'I'm sorry to disappoint you, *cara*, but I am certainly not friendless.'

'But your stepsister of all people. She *knows* we are fakes!'

His mood changed in a flicker. 'Stop playing the scared innocent, Rachel, when we both know you are far from it,' he clipped out. 'This is what you signed up for to save your sister's marriage. And lovers who fall on one other as often as we do are certainly not faking it!'

She pushed her hands through her hair. 'You know what I meant.'

'And you know what I mean when I say—get your act together,' he instructed, 'because we are going out in public tonight and I want the besotted *lover* by my side, not the farmer with a chip on her shoulder a mile wide!'

Rachel stared at him. 'What's that supposed to imply?'

He threw out an impatient hand. 'You compare yourself badly to your more glamorous sister,' he provided. 'You compare me with your ex-lover and hate the fact that I am Italian like him.'

'I do not!' she denied.

'Was he good-looking?' he demanded.

'What has that got to do with anything?' Her eyes went wide in bewilderment.

'Was he—?' he persisted.

'Yes!'

'How old?'

'My age—'

'And what kind of car did he drive?'

She sucked in an angry breath. 'A red Ferrari,' she answered. 'But that wasn't—'

'Great,' he gritted. 'Mine is silver. Is that a bad mark against me or one against him for being too flashy?'

'You're crazy,' she breathed.

Maybe he was. At this precise moment Raffaelle did not know why he was so fired up about a man he probably would not give a second thought to in other circumstances.

'Just go and get ready.' He turned his back on her and strode into his study, wanting to toss his drink to the back of his angry throat but refusing to allow himself the gut soothing pleasure while she was standing there staring at him. 'And I *don't* like flashy, so don't come out dressed in red!' he could not stop himself from adding.

Then he shut the door—*slammed* the damn door!

Rachel shook all the way into the bedroom. She shook as she removed her coat and laid it aside. She had absolutely no idea what all of that had been about and she didn't think that she wanted to know.

Did he hate her—was that it? she immediately questioned. Did he resent her being here so badly that he needed to take chunks out of her to get his own back on her for putting him in this situation in the first place?

Was he locked in his silly study *praying* that she wasn't pregnant with his child?

And he did not want to see the farmer dressed in flashy red when she came out. Her lips gave a quiver. He preferred to see the sleek Elise look-alike because at least he could relate to her and *pretend* she was his type!

Rachel stripped off her clothes and walked into the bathroom, not sure if she wanted to throw things or cry her eyes out.

The tears almost won the moment she stepped beneath the shower spray and she would have let them if he had not chosen that moment to push open the bathroom door and stride fully naked into the shower.

'No, don't stiffen up,' he said as she did exactly that. 'I am here to make you feel better, not worse.'

He drew her back against him, angling both of them so the shower sprayed down her front, then dropped his lips to her ear. 'I came to apologise for being bad-tempered out there.'

'You mean it's just hit you that you have to trail me in front of your friends having ripped my head off,' Rachel said.

'I had a bad day.'

He was tasting her earlobe now. Rachel jerked it away.

'Accepting invitations you had no desire to accept.'

'While thinking of you and that bed I had walked away from.' He chased the earlobe again. 'So I was bad tempered all day and came home more than ready to find you waiting for me. But you were not here; you were out enjoying yourself.'

'Playing the farmer to my heart's content.'

'I like the farmer,' he murmured lustily. 'She is toned and sleek and very sexy. I am also jealous of the ex-lover…'

That shocking confession finally stopped her from trying to pull away from him.

'Impressed by that?' he mocked.

'Yes,' she answered honestly.

'I thought you might be.' His mouth bit gently into the sensitive crook between her shoulder and neck.

Rachel's breathing feathered and she closed her eyes, giving herself up to this when she knew that she shouldn't. Wanting him to want her for herself and not just because she was here for the taking.

He found the soap and used it to paint every inch of her he could reach. Soon she was lost in a scented steam-filled world that shut out everything else.

Afterwards she felt lazy and languid and much too aware of him as her irresistible lover as the two of them moved around between the bathroom, bedroom and dressing room, preparing to go out.

Which had been the object of the exercise in the shower, she reminded herself. Several times he stopped her passing him by just fusing his mouth to hers in a slow clinging kiss and the lazily hooded way in which he watched her shyly lower her eyes and move away quickly only heightened an intimacy that was threatening to take her over completely if she didn't watch out.

She was relieved when he finally left her alone so she could finish getting ready without having him around as such a breathtaking distraction. By the time she joined him in the living room Rachel truly believed she had managed to get herself together—until he looked up from the broadsheet newspaper he was reading while lounging on a sofa and the whole whirlwind of awareness whipped into action again.

She'd chosen to wear a sleek short V-neck dress in dramatic matt black. Elise had donated the dress, claiming that it did not suit her because she didn't have the curves to fill it out.

Well, Rachel had the curves and, the way that Raffaelle was looking at her, he had not missed a single one. Her hair was loose, its curls carefully ironed out so the style was smooth and sleek. As he rose to his feet her blue eyes followed him, defiant yet anxious—just in case she did not look as good as she hoped she did.

But the look reassured her as he came towards her wearing the kind of black lounge suit that yelled couture *homme*. When an Italian male dressed he never ever dressed badly, was Rachel's single dry-mouthed heart pummelling observation.

'Beautiful,' he murmured as he reached her,

sending pleasurable shivers chasing up her spine as he bent to brush a caress on her cheek. 'But I prefer the curls.'

'Different woman,' she answered with a small shrug.

His eyes narrowed, all the sensuality hardened out of his mouth. He said nothing for several long seconds and Rachel knew she had just managed to remind him of the real reason why they were together.

Maybe that was a good thing, she decided, as he helped her into the little black satin evening jacket she had brought into the room with her, still without saying anything else. They left the apartment and travelled in the lift down to where Dino waited by the car with the rear passenger door open. She slid in. The door clicked shut. Raffaelle rounded the bonnet and slid in from the other side. His long body folded with crease-free elegance into the seat beside her.

Lean, sleek, supremely sophisticated, she recognised. Crossing one silk-covered knee over the other, she fixed her attention on the partition which separated them from Dino.

Tension fizzed in the silence. Rachel found herself clinging to her little black beaded purse.

The car swished along London's busy streets, recently drenched by a heavy downpour of rain. Everything outside the car seemed to glitter and sparkle in the darkness, everything inside the car was shadowed and oddly flat.

Raffaelle wished he knew what he was feeling right now, but he didn't. It was crazy to have been so taken aback by her reminder of what this was all about when they'd done little else but argue about it since they'd first met.

But he had been taken aback by it, stunned by the gut-twisting reminder that none of this was real—that *she* wasn't real.

Not tonight anyway.

She was the sleek look-alike sister of Elise Castle-Savakis, pretending to be a version of Rachel Carmichael that just did not exist. Even the dress was Elise's, classy and stylish and very sexy on Rachel, but he would be prepared to bet it was not of her own taste or choice.

He preferred the other Rachel with the curls and the spark of defiance in her blue eyes.

'Having second thoughts about risking me in there amongst your friends?' she asked suddenly.

Raffaelle blinked, realising that they'd come to a stop outside the restaurant. By the atmosphere inside the car, they'd been here like this for several seconds.

The restaurant was one of the best Italian restaurants in London. It was a place where the rich set ate. It was his kind of place and his kind of life, but neither were hers.

He turned his head to look at her. Barely an hour ago, she had been coming all around him in a breathtaking pulse of intimacy that still circulated in his blood. He looked at her silk-straight hair and her beautiful pearly-white complexion, the heavily accentuated black-lashed blue eyes and the sexy pink-coated mouth.

He could taste them. He could feel those soft pink-coated lips warm against his own whether she was this Rachel or the other Rachel. And if he was sitting here like this, wanting to know where the two Rachels became one, then he'd found it in that mouth and what happened to her when he claimed it.

'I won't embarrass you, if that's what's worrying you,' she stated, fizzing inside with resentment at the analytical way he was looking her over as if he was actually having to give some deep thought to the sarcastic question she had tossed out.

'You sound very sure about that, little farmer girl,' he said huskily.

'Well, I'm not,' she admitted honestly. 'I suppose I should have said I will *try* not to embarrass you.'

Easing his wide shoulders into the corner of the seat, his eyes glittered over her tense face. 'Do you really believe I will care if you do decide to embarrass me?' he asked curiously.

Rachel offered a shrug. 'I don't know you well enough to judge.'

'No, you don't…'

She didn't like the way he had said that, or the way he was looking at her now. Her tension was zinging along just about every nerve ending she had in her body and she wished he would just—

'Are we going to go in there or not?' she flicked out.

'In a minute,' he said smoothly, 'This conversation is just getting interesting…'

'No, it isn't.'

'Because it has nothing to do with whether you are going to embarrass me,' he said ignoring her interruption. 'It is to do with you being scared that I might embarrass you.'

Rachel stared at him. 'Why should you want to do that?'

'My thought exactly,' he said softly. 'Yet you *are* scared that I am going to take you in there, then just leave you to sink or swim.'

Her pink upper lip gave a vulnerable quiver. 'I was thinking more along the lines of being served up along with the main course,' she confessed.

He laughed. It was bad of him. But it was a very low, sexily-amused laugh and Rachel laughed too—one of those tense little sounds that jump up unexpectedly from the throat.

The atmosphere changed in that single moment, spinning the tension into a fine thread that eddied across the gap between them then morphed into something else. He moved so fast that she didn't see him coming, and then it was too late when he had taken arrogant possession of her mouth.

'You've stolen all my lipstick,' she protested when the kiss came to an end.

'I know.' He sat back a little, watching her as she fumbled in her bag for a tissue and her lipstick case. 'Keep on reapplying it, *cara*,' he advised as she re-applied a coating of pink with a decidedly unsteady hand. 'Because I find I like doing it. In fact I do believe I am becoming addicted to the taste.'

She handed him the tissue. 'It looks better on me than it does on you.'

And he grinned, wiping pink from his lips while his eyes tangled with hers. It was no use pretending that they weren't doing something else here, because they were.

Then suddenly he was being serious. 'Listen to me,' he urged. 'I don't want you to be anyone but yourself tonight, okay? I don't care if you want to spend the evening going on about the pros of organic produce. I don't care if you decide to ruffle your hair into curls or you march off to the kitchens to tout the chef for his business—'

'I'm not quite that uncouth!' she cried.

'You are missing the point,' he chided. 'The point being that I don't give a damn if you are just yourself and act like yourself. The only thing I do care about is that you stick to the main story as to how we met and keep in mind that, when we leave here, we go home to my apartment together as a couple, then to bed and to—this.'

Another kiss was on its way to her. 'Don't you dare,' Rachel drew her head back.

But he did dare—quickly, briefly, not enough to steal her lipstick a second time but more than enough to distract her from what he was about to do next.

She felt her left hand being taken. By the time she

had the sense to glance down, the fake sapphire ring had been removed and he was already replacing it with one that looked exactly the same.

'W-what have you done that for?' she demanded.

'The fake might have been a good fake, *cara*, but it did not stand a chance of fooling the experts we are about to meet.'

'It fooled you when you saw it.' She was staring at the exact copy now adorning her finger.

'I was too angry to notice it then.'

'It's so—gaudy.' She sighed, staring at the ring as it shimmered and sparkled much more than its predecessor.

'Not to your taste?'

'Not to anyone's taste,' she said ruefully. 'It was only meant to grab Leo's attention… How did you get hold of this one so quickly?'

'I am the kind of man who gets what he wants when he wants it,' he answered with careless conceit.

He went to put the fake ring into his pocket.

'No—' As quick as a flash Rachel plucked it from his hand and pushed it into her beaded purse. 'I'll wear the real one when we are out together, but only then,' she informed him stubbornly. 'Otherwise I'll wear the fake one.'

'If you're afraid of losing it, it is insured—'

But Rachel gave a shake of her head. This had nothing to do with losing the real ring, but more to do with the fear that if she didn't hang on to the fake she would lose touch with reality.

'I will only wear it when we are out,' she repeated.

'And in our bed?' he demanded shortly.

Rachel thought about that for a second or two. 'I won't wear either ring,' she decided.

'Meaning our sexual relationship has nothing to do with the rest of this?'

Unless he was able to fake what was happening there as well. Then she nodded, because the sex was the only truly honest part of this.

He said nothing but just sighed and went to open the car door—then suddenly changed his mind. He turned on her, caught her chin in his fingers, then dipped his head for a third, definite, lipstick-stealing, full-blooded, possessive lover's kiss.

'The sexual part of this relationship does not stay behind in the bedroom, Rachel,' he stated harshly. 'Remember that, while you fix your lipstick again…'

He climbed out of the car then, leaving her sitting there trembling and shaken by the anger which had erupted from him.

What was the matter with him? Why should he care which ring she wore, so long as she didn't make *him* look the cheap fake?

Her lips felt tender and bruised this time as she reapplied the lipstick. He'd walked around the car and was now standing with her door open, waiting for her to join him on the pavement.

It was chilly outside and her satin jacket had not been made to keep the cold out. She shivered. He stepped closer, fitting her beneath his shoulder and curling his hand into her waist.

Gosh, don't we look the picture of romance? she thought dryly as he walked her towards the restaurant.

'Smile,' he instructed as he pushed the door open.

Rachel looked up to find that he was looking down at her. One of those frozen in time moments suddenly grabbed them, locking them inside their own private space.

'Heavens, Raffaelle,' another voice intruded. 'You were out there so long we were about to lay bets as to whether or not you were going to just take her back home again.'

'As you see, Daniella,' he came back smoothly, 'Rachel's manners are so much better than mine...'

He held Rachel's eyes as he said it. He watched

her cheeks warm to a blush when she realised what Daniella had meant. Then he took hold of her hand and lifted it to his lips. The engagement ring sparkled as he kissed it. Her soft pink pulsing mouth gave a telling little quiver that shot an injection of heat down to his groin.

Someone else spoke—he did not know who. When he turned, he could barely make sense of the blur of faces all smiling at them.

What the hell was the matter with him? Was he sickening for something to have double-vision like this? It would be the first germ to catch him out since his childhood, he mused grimly, frowning as he looked back at Rachel.

Her face was in perfect focus. He did not like what that discovery was trying to say to him. With a taut shift of his shoulders, he pulled himself together and turned to face his dinner guests again, then switched on his lazy smile.

'*Buona sera*,' he greeted. 'My apologies for keeping you waiting when I know you are dying to meet my beautiful Rachel…'

CHAPTER NINE

MY BEAUTIFUL Rachel...

And so began the worst evening of his beautiful Rachel's life.

Raffaelle's stepsister did not believe a single word that either of them said to her. The others were more than happy to welcome her into their set, but they too were surprised and curious about this complete stranger who had arrived out of nowhere into Raffaelle's life.

Rachel supposed she should be relieved that Daniella seemed to have kept her suspicions to herself—or maybe she was too scared of Raffaelle to actually say what she thought outright. But she quizzed Rachel mercilessly about Elise.

'How is she?'

'Wonderful, taking a holiday in Florida with her husband and son.'

'You two met through Elise?'

'No, we met at a dinner party given by friends of Leo and Elise.'

Daniella had eyes like bitter chocolate which constantly flicked from Rachel to Raffaelle. 'Both of you were very secretive about this romance.'

'Rachel liked it that way,' her stepbrother answered. '*We* liked it that way. Look at what happened the moment we were seen in public. It turned into a witch-hunt.'

'When a woman throws herself at you in front of a reporter, it tends to have that effect. So does standing naked in a bedroom window.'

Rachel flushed but Raffaelle remained completely unruffled. 'Behaving like a spoiled child who does not like to know she has been left out of a secret is very unappealing,' he responded lightly.

Reducing her to the level of a spoiled child may have silenced Daniella but it did not kill her suspicions about Rachel not being who she claimed she was—as she made very clear the moment she got Rachel alone in the ladies' room.

'I *know* he was seeing Elise Castle because it was me who told him she was married with a small son! So don't try to pull the wool over my eyes, Miss Carmichael. That ring is a fake, just as everything else about you is fake.'

Rachel looked down at the sparkling diamond and sapphire cluster adorning her finger and grimaced. 'I don't want to fight with you, Daniella—'

'Well, I want to fight with you,' Daniella said fiercely. 'I *saw* you throw yourself at Raffaelle the other night. I *saw* his rage. I think you and Elise are trying to blackmail him!'

Apart from the fact that she was so close to the truth it was scary, Rachel had to feel for Daniella if only because she looked and sounded so worried and protective of Raffaelle.

'And you aren't drinking alcohol!' Daniella said suddenly. 'Are you pregnant, is that it? Did you have a fling with him, as well as your sister, and now you're demanding marriage?'

Rachel stared at the other girl as if she had just grown two heads. Was she psychic or what? 'I don't drink.' She iced out the lie with as much calmness as she could. 'And repeat your accusations to Raffaelle, if you dare,' she challenged.

Then she turned and walked out of the ladies' room. Raffaelle took one look at her flushed angry face and stood up before she could sit down.

His arms came around her. 'Problems?' he asked.

Rachel shook her head, aware of the others listening. 'Just a—headache,' she offered as a very weak excuse.

'Then we will leave.'

It was not a suggestion and Rachel did not argue with him. As they made their farewells Daniella came back to the table. One slicing glance at her stepbrother and her chin shot up in defiance.

To make everything feel even worse, a camera flashed as Raffaelle was helping Rachel on with her jacket. He'd lowered his head to kiss the side of her neck in one of those loving displays he'd been putting on all evening.

'What was it with Daniella?' he demanded the moment they were back in the car.

'She knows,' she responded.

'She knows what?'

'Everything,' she answered heavily. 'She thinks I'm blackmailing you over your affair with Elise.'

'You were blackmailing me,' he pointed out dryly.

'She also accused me of being pregnant because I wasn't drinking tonight, and of having a fling with you at the same time you were with Elise.' She grimaced. 'Great reputation you have there, *Signor*, when even your own family can believe you are capable of swinging it with two women at the same time.'

'She's fishing for information, that's all,' he answered coolly. 'And she—cares about me.'

'Lucky you,' Rachel mumbled.

'Do you say that because your family shows so little concern for you?'

That hit her right below the belt. 'My family care,' she insisted.

'Your uncle, maybe,' Raffaelle conceded. 'But even he made the quick getaway once he believed he had established that I was not your heart-breaker from Naples. I could have been lying to him. He did not hang around long enough to put me to the test.'

'He's a busy man.' She shifted tensely on the seat next to him.

'Like your half-sister and -brother are so busy they have not had time to check if I have chopped you into little pieces and dumped you in the Thames?'

'Sh-shut up,' she breathed.

They finished the rest of the journey in silence. As they travelled up in the lift to Rafaelle's apartment, Rachel stared fixedly down at her feet and he—well, she didn't know what he was looking at but she had an itchy feeling it could be her.

Once inside the apartment she headed for one

of the spare bedrooms because there was just no way she was going to sleep with him tonight.

He didn't try to stop her, which only stressed her out more. She slept restlessly beneath a navy-blue duvet wearing only her bra and panties, woke up early the next morning and remade the bed, then crept back into the other bedroom to get some fresh clothes before Rosa arrived.

The plum-covered bed was empty and, by the look of it, Raffaelle had enjoyed a restless night too. She glanced at the closed bathroom door to listen if the shower was running, hoping to goodness that he'd already got up and dressed and taken himself off to work and out of the firing line.

'Discovered your sense of fair play, *amore*?' a smooth voice murmured.

She spun around to find him standing in the dressing room doorway wearing only a towel slung low around his hips. It was like being hit by that high wattage charge again.

'I—thought you would have left by now,' she said without thinking.

He just smiled then began walking forward. Rachel started to back away.

'Slept well?' he asked her.

'Yes, thank you.'

'Need any help tying that robe?'

She glanced down, then released a gasp when she saw the robe she had pinched from the other bathroom was hanging open revealingly. It was too big, a man's full-length heavy towelling bathrobe that trailed the floor at her feet and engulfed her hands. She'd thought she'd tied the belt, but the stupid thing had slid undone.

'Go away,' she shook out, trying to fight with the sleeves so she could grab the two ends of the belt.

But Raffaelle Villani wasn't going anywhere. He just kept coming until he was standing right in front of her. Then, while she mumbled out a protest, he pushed her fingers away and calmly cinched the belt around her waist. His fingers brushed the skin of her stomach as he did it. She breathed in sharply. He ignored the revealing breath, finished his task, then calmly turned away, dropping the towel from around his hips, and strode like the arrogant man he was back into the dressing room and closed the door.

It was the same as a slap in the face. She refused to sleep with him and he was showing her that it made little difference to him.

Rachel ran into the bathroom and wished she was dead, because her body was such a quivering mass of frustration that if he'd stripped the robe from her and thrown her to the bed, she would not have stopped him.

Her day was long and she was tired by the time she trailed into the apartment again. Rosa had gone home hours ago. Raffaelle was still out, which allowed her some time for herself to take a long bath behind a firmly locked bathroom door in an effort to relax some of the tension grinding at her every nerve and muscle.

She stayed in the bath longer than she'd meant to. By the time she let herself back into the bedroom she could sense more than hear that Raffaelle was home, though he was not in the bedroom, thank goodness, which gave her a chance to pull her jeans back on and a fresh T-shirt before she heaved in a breath and went looking for him.

He was in the kitchen making himself a sandwich, the jacket to his suit gone, white shirt-sleeves rolled up. He turned at the sound of her step. Her stomach dipped. She found herself running self conscious fingers through her curls.

'*Ciao*,' he said lightly. 'You look—pink.'

'I stayed in the bath too long,' she explained as naturally as she could.

He turned back to what he was doing. 'Want a sandwich?'

Her stomach gave a hungry growl. 'What's in it?'

'Take your pick,' he invited, pointing to the variety of salad things he had already sliced up. 'There's cheese in the fridge, some chicken and ham.'

Choosing the ham because she saw it first, she took over and handed it to him. Then surprised herself by staying there watching as he layered fresh bread with salad stuff.

'Not going to offer to do it for me?' He arched a look at her.

'Not me,' she said. 'I might grow the produce but I can't cook it,' she confessed. 'Ask me to make a sandwich like that and it will fall apart the moment you pick it up.'

'No culinary skills at all, then.'

'Not a single one.'

'Any good with a coffee machine?'

'Hit and miss.' She grimaced. 'I'm an instant coffee girl.'

'Tragic,' he murmured. 'Give it a try anyway.' He nodded to where the coffee machine stood. 'It's loaded and ready to hit the cup like the instant stuff does, only it tastes better.'

'That's an Italian opinion.' She moved across to

the machine and fed it a cup as she'd done two days before.

Two days, she then thought suddenly—they felt like years. How had that happened?

'Tony tells me you have been treading the miles again,' he murmured.

She turned to look at him curiously. 'How often does he report in to you?'

The wide shoulders gave a shrug inside expensive white shirting that didn't quite stop the gold of his skin from showing through. 'Each time you stop somewhere.'

'Do you think it's necessary? I mean, I haven't seen a glimpse of a reporter in the two days I've been out and about.'

'Then you would make a lousy detective.' Turning he pointed to the newspaper lying on the table.

Going over to it, Rachel saw a photo of herself sitting at a table in a top Knightsbridge restaurant drinking morning coffee with its famous chef owner. A flush arrived on her cheeks because, not only was she aware that she had not seen the lurking reporter but she'd now realised that the only reason why she had been sitting there at all was because the chef had recognised her and his curiosity had been piqued.

'Where was Tony when this was taken?' she demanded. It was his job after all to stop this from happening.

'He did clear the reporter off, but not before he had managed to take this one photograph. Then the guy waited until you had left the restaurant and went back to quiz the chef.'

The chef had given an interview, getting a plug for his restaurant by happily telling the reporter what Rachel Carmichael did for a living. There was another photograph in a different paper showing Raffaelle kissing her cheek as he helped her on with her jacket.

'What it is to be famous,' she murmured cynically.

'Well, your secret other life is now out,' Raffaelle declared. 'Which means you can stop hiding behind the mask of Elise when we go out.'

'Daniella is going to love it.'

He turned with two loaded plates in his hands. 'I've spoken to Daniella.'

Rachel froze as he put the plates down on the table.

'She sends you her apologies and promises to behave the next time that you meet.'

'She had nothing to apologise to me for,' Rachel said flatly. 'Actually, I could like her despite...'

'Daniella not liking you?'

'Yes,' she said huskily.

He pulled out a chair and sat down on it. 'You can tell her you like her later when we meet up at the theatre—'

'*Theatre*—?' Rachel stared at him. 'I don't want to go to the theatre!'

'Sit down and eat,' he instructed. 'If you are eating for two you must have a good balanced diet.'

Rachel stared slack-jawed at him.

Steady-eyed, Raffaelle just shrugged. 'I'm the fatalist, remember? I work through problems sometimes before they are problems. It is what helps to keep me at the top.'

'You're not short on insufferable arrogance either. You and Daniella should share the same blood.'

He just grinned over the top of his sandwich. 'Tell me why you don't want to go to the theatre,' he instructed.

She pulled out a chair and sat down on it. 'I don't get the opportunity to go often enough to get to like it.'

'Well, that's about to change.'

'What kind of theatre?' she asked dubiously.

'Opera,' he provided. As her jaw dropped again,

he said, 'Get used to it because it is the love of my life. Eat.'

Rachel picked up her sandwich. It arrived by instinct at her mouth because her eyes certainly didn't guide it there—they were still looking at him in horrified disbelief.

'I can't believe you want to put me through an *opera*,' she protested.

'We either go to the opera or we stay in and make love…'

And, just like that, their few minutes of near normality disappeared without a trace.

Rachel put down the sandwich. He chewed on his, his eyes gleaming with challenge.

'I'm will *not* be blackmailed into your bed—!' She flew to her feet.

'Then prepare for an evening of Tosca,' he countered coolly. 'Wear something long and—sexy. Oh, and take your sandwich with you, *mi amore*,' he drawled as she went to flounce out of the room. 'The opera starts early and supper will be late.'

She wore a long slender blue gown that faithfully followed her every curve. Raffaelle took one look at her and staked possessive claim with a hand to the indentation of her waist.

'*Mine*,' he declared huskily. 'Make sure you remember it while we are out.'

Sitting for hours beside a man who seemed to take pleasure in playing the deeply besotted lover throughout the interminable though admittedly moving music heightened her senses to such a degree that she had never felt more relieved to walk out into the ice-cold evening air so she could breathe.

They ate supper with a crowd of people including Daniella, who was quieter than the night before and was almost pleasant to Rachel, though Rachel could tell by the glint in the other woman's brown eyes that the pleasantness ran only skin-deep. Daniella was still suspicious and hostile and hungered for the real truth as to what was going on.

Rachel gave Daniella no chance of getting her on her own that evening, staying put in her seat and keeping her attention fixed on everyone else. At least they seemed to accept her at face value—it was difficult not to when the man sitting beside her rarely took his eyes from her face. Tension zinged between them like static. Rachel refused to so much as glance at him, smiling where she thought she should do and trying to ignore the ever increasing pulse of awareness he was making her suffer. She was quizzed about her occupation and it seemed a good time to launch into the benefits of organic farming with an enthusiastic vigour that set such an animated debate going she almost managed to forget Raffaelle was sitting there.

Then he reached out to gently take hold of her chin and turned it so she had no choice but to look at him. His expression was difficult to read, kind of mocking yet deadly serious at the same time.

'You are here with me,' he said huskily.

'I know who I'm with.' She frowned at him.

'Then don't ignore me.'

'I wasn't ignoring you. I was—'

'Smiling at every other man at this table but me.'

The idea that he might be feeling left out and jealous sent a different kind of sting singing through her blood. Her eyes must have showed it because his thumb arrived to rub across her lower lip in an intimate, very sexual proclamation that brought a telling flush to her cheeks.

But she could not pull back or break eye contact. It was too much like being plugged into an electric current again—lit up from the inside and sensually enlivened. He knew it, he built it until her breathing quickened and her eyes darkened. She could feel Daniella watching them. She heard someone else murmur dryly, 'Time to break up the party, I think.'

'Good idea,' he murmured and leant forward to replace the thumb with his mouth in a brief promise of a kiss that brought him smoothly to his feet.

They travelled back to his apartment in absolute silence. They rode the lift in exactly the same way. Rachel kept her eyes fixed on her feet again but refusing to look at him did not ease the sexual pull taking place. They walked along the hallway towards the bedrooms still accompanied by that highly strung clamour of perfect silence.

When they reached the door to his bedroom they paused. Still he said nothing and still she was fighting it until—

'Well—?' he asked softly.

Rachel drew in a tense, sizzling, battling breath, tried to let it out again but found that she couldn't. Her senses were singing out a chant of surrender and in the end she gave in to it, turning to reach for the door handle to his bedroom.

Without saying a single word he followed her inside and closed the door. Now she'd made the decision to come in here she did not go for modesty but just turned to face him and, with the light of a looming sexual battle lighting her blue eyes, she began to undress right there in front of him. His face was deadly serious as he watched her for a few seconds before he began to undress too.

Clothes landed on the floor all around them. Her dress pooled in a slither of blue silk at her feet. It was all part of the battle that they did not break eye contact.

Rachel walked towards the bed on legs that no longer wished to support her. Indeed they preferred to tingle and sting like the rest of her body, making sure they did not give her a moment to change her mind about this.

No chance—no *hope* of a last-minute reprieve. She wanted him so badly she couldn't think beyond the need.

He took up a position on the other side of the bed and the tip of her tongue crept out to curl across her upper lip as she let her eyes glide over him. Big, lean, hard and aroused. Her breasts grew heavy and her nipples peaked, the wall of muscle around her lower stomach contracting as she tried to contain the ache.

She lifted the duvet. He did the same. They slid into the bed together and arrived in the middle of the mattress in a limb-tangling clasp of body contact.

Then he kissed her. No, he punished her for putting them through twenty-four hours of denial.

That night Rachel learned what it was like to be totally taken over, excruciatingly sapped of her will by a man with a magician's touch. He wove sensual spells around every pleasure point. He drove her wild until she cried out. Then he possessed her, deep, tough and ruthlessly, staking claim in this final act of ownership that had her clinging and trembling and sobbing out his name as she tumbled into release.

And so began four hellish weeks trapped inside heaven.

When Raffaelle had said they were to be as if they were glued together, he'd meant it. Wherever his business took him, Rachel went with him, hopping from London to Milan, Paris, Monaco then back to London then Milan again. In one short month she learned what it was like to become a fully paid-up member of the jet set and how it felt to be recognised as the woman who'd managed to pin the very eligible Raffaelle Villani down.

Everywhere they went he took her out into public places—more restaurants, more theatres, nightclubs and private parties—all very select venues where they could be displayed as a couple.

It was almost all glitz and glamour. There were those in his close circle of friends who were the kind of people she could relate to mainly because they were easy to like. Then there were the other kind who hovered on the fringes of it all who would have sold their grandmothers to be included as a member of his inner set.

Then there was the seemingly endless stream of his ex-lovers from all over the world who had no problem with telling her what they used to be to him and thought it fine to discuss the ins and outs of having a lover like him.

'Have they never heard of the word discretion?' she tossed at him after one particularly vocal beauty had seen nothing wrong in singing his sexual praises to Rachel—in front of Raffaelle. 'Or does it stroke your ego to hear someone talk about you as if you were a stallion put out to stud and therefore free to be debated for your sexual prowess?'

'I don't like it,' he denied.

'Then don't smile that smug smile while they list your assets.'

'It is not a smug smile, it is a forbearing one. And you sound like a jealously disapproving wife.'

'No, just a lover who does not think you are so great in bed that you deserve so much attention,' she denounced.

'No—?'

She should have read the intimation in that *no* but she missed it.

'No,' she repeated.

'Maybe you found the Italian heartbreaker and sex tutor of innocents a better lover?'

She turned icy eyes on him. 'If you're fishing for information, then forget it. Unlike your ex-lovers, this one does not kiss and tell.'

He had been fishing for information, Raffaelle acknowledged. She might be the best lover he'd ever enjoyed but he had no clue as to where she placed him on her admittedly short list.

And he'd accused her of being jealous when he knew that was his issue. Jealous, curious, wary of the way she sometimes looked at him as if he was a being from outer space. Their age difference bothered him. Her youth and her beauty and that softer side she had to her that made some of his previous women appear sex-hardened and clinical. Did she see *him* like that: sex-hardened and clinical?

His male friends were drawn to her. He did not

like to see it because he knew exactly what it was about her that drew them. They wanted to experience what he was experiencing. They wanted to know what it felt like to simply touch a woman like Rachel and have her melt softly for them.

And she did melt. It was his only source of male satisfaction. In company, out of company, he touched her and she melted. He *looked* at her and she melted.

'Well, remember that I am the lover who takes you to heaven each night,' he said.

And, like Alonso, Rachel knew that he would break her heart one day.

He obsessed her mind and her body. She hated him sometimes, but her desire for him was stronger than hate. He knew it too and the inner battles she fought with herself turned him on. She watched it happen, watched right up until the moment they reached the lift which would take them into privacy and saw the social face he wore fall away to reveal the hard, dark, sexually intense man.

The lift became her torture chamber. The stinging strikes of his sexual promise flayed her skin. By the time they stepped through his front door she was a minefield of electric impulses, hardly breathing, hyped up and charged beyond anything sane.

Sometimes he would crash into that minefield right there in the hallway. Sometimes he would draw out the agony by making her wait before he unleashed the sensual storm. She learned to live on a high wire of expectation that allowed no respite and little sleep, with him even invading her dreams.

He knew every single sensitive inch of her. Sometimes he would coax her to stretch out on the bed with her arms raised above her and her legs pressed together, then he'd begin a long slow torture that she loved yet hated with equal passion because he would make her come—eventually— with only the lightest stroke of a finger or the gentlest flicker of his tongue. It was an un- ashamed act of male domination which left her aching because he never gave in to his own need on these occasions or finished such torments off with an intimate, deep physical joining.

Why did he do that? Even after four weeks with him she still did not have an answer to that question.

And then there were those other times. The times when he allowed her to perform the same slow torment on him. He would lie there with his eyes closed and his long body taut with sexual tension while she indulged her every whim.

Being equals, he called it. She called it dangerous, because it had reached a stage where she could not look at him without seeing him lost in the throes of what he was feeling on those occasions. A big golden man, trembling and vulnerable, a slave to what she could make him feel.

The elixir which kept her rooted in their relationship, wanting—needing more.

And other things began to torment her which were far more disturbing than the constant overwhelming heat of desire. She knew she had fallen in love with him. She could feel it tugging constantly at the vulnerable muscles around her heart. If he touched her those muscles squeezed and quivered. If she let her eyes rest on him, those same muscles dipped into a sinking tingling dive.

But Raffaelle was not in this for love. He wanted her, yes. He still desired her so fiercely that she would have to be a complete idiot not to know that he was content to keep things the way they were right now.

If she had any sense she would be walking away from it. Elise and Leo were back in Chicago. Elise was happy, Leo was happy and keeping his pregnant wife and his son close to him; the crisis in their marriage was over.

All of this should be over now. And, if it wasn't for the worrying prospect that her period was overdue, she would have no excuse left to call upon which could allow her to stay.

Then it all went so spectacularly pear-shaped that it threw everything they had together into a reeling spin.

They were in Milan when it happened. Raffaelle was tense, distant, preoccupied—busy with an important deal, he said. But Rachel wondered if the stress of waiting to discover if she was pregnant was getting to him too.

He didn't say so—never mentioned it at all and neither did she.

She knew that she needed to buy a pregnancy test. Putting it off any longer was silly when she was almost a whole week late. She was supposed to be going shopping with one of Raffaelle's many cousins but Carlotta had rung up to say she couldn't make it.

On impulse she snatched up her purse and headed out of the apartment. She should have called Tony to get him to drive her, but she didn't want anyone with her to witness what she was going to do.

She caught a cab into the city, then headed for a row of shops that included a pharmacy. Anxiety kept her locked inside her own thoughts as she walked, but the last thing she expected to happen was to be woken from them by a loud screech of brakes as a glossy red open top Ferrari swished to a sudden stop at her side,

The man driving that car did not bother to open the door to climb out but leapt with lithe limbed grace over the door. 'Rachel—*amore*!' he called out.

Shock held her completely frozen, her blue gaze fixed on his familiar handsome face.

'Alonso—?' she gasped in surprise.

'*Si*—!' He laughed, all flashing white teeth, black silk hair and honey-gold beauty. 'Is this not the greatest surprise of your life?'

CHAPTER TEN

HE BEGAN closing the gap between them, a lean muscled six-foot-two inch-Italian encased in the finest silver-grey suit. A man with so much natural charisma and self-belief that it just would not occur to him that he was anything but a welcome sight to her.

So Rachel found herself engulfed by the pair of arms he folded around her, then found herself being kissed on her cheeks and the tip of her nose, then her surprised, still parted mouth.

She tried to pull back but he was not letting her. 'I saw you get out of a cab and I could not believe my eyes!' he exclaimed. 'And look at you,' he murmured, running a teasing set of fingers through the bouncy curls on her head. 'Still my beautiful Rachel.' He kissed her mouth again. 'This has to be the best moment of my day!'

Well, not mine, thought Rachel, still rolling on

the shock of seeing him. 'What are you doing here in Milan?'

'I could ask the same thing of you.' He grinned down at her. 'Though I would have to be blind not to know by now that you have captured the heart of Raffaelle Villani, eh? May good fortune always smile upon the bewitching,' he proposed expansively. 'He is totally besotted with you, as I was, of course…'

Across the street, on the shady side, sitting languidly at a lunch table with five business associates, Raffaelle happened to glance outside in time to see Rachel walking by on the sunny side of the street.

A smile warmed him from the inside. She looked beautiful in her simple white top and her short blue skirt which left a pleasurable amount of her long legs bare. And her silky blonde hair was shining in the sunlight, recently cut by an expert so the curls tumbled around her neck and her face like sensual kisses.

It was no wonder other men stopped to admire her as she walked past them, he observed, a smile catching the corners of his mouth as he saw one guy in particular actually spin around to take a second look.

Sorry, but she belongs exclusively to me, he

heard himself stake the silent claim. Then he started to frown when another thought hit him. Where was Tony? Where was his cousin Carlotta? Why was Rachel out shopping alone when she knew the rules about going out without protection from the ever-watchful press?

The sound of screeching car brakes diverted his attention. A glossy red Ferrari with its top down had pulled to a sudden stop in the street. Its handsome young owner leapt out with lean grace and approached Rachel with his arms thrown open.

She had stopped to stare at him. What took place next lost Raffaelle the power to maintain a grip on his surroundings. The quiet hum of conversation taking place around the lunch table disappeared from his consciousness as he saw her soft pink mouth frame a name.

The man spoke, his gestures expressive, like the rakish smile he delivered as he gathered her into his arms, then kissed her cheeks, her nose and finally, lingeringly, her parted pink mouth.

A mouth that belonged to *him*. A mouth that did not attempt to draw back from the kiss.

So cold he felt frozen now, Raffaelle watched this other man run his fingers through her curls as he talked.

Small, familiar, intimate gestures. Soft parted pink lips that quivered when she spoke back to him.

They knew each other.

His heart hit his gut because it did not take much intelligence to follow the body language and know without a single hint of doubt who the man had to be.

Alonso. The heartbreaker. He was so sure of it he did not even think to question his certainty.

Had they arranged to meet—right here in broad daylight without a care as to who might see them like this?

How long had they been in touch with each other? Each time he had brought her with him here to Milan?

Was she still in love with him?

Dio. While she stood there in his arms, looking up at him like that, was her heart beating too fast and her throat drying up and her blue eyes helplessly drinking him in?

'Raffaelle…'

The sound of his name being spoken finally sank into his consciousness. Turning his head, he received the impression that it was not the first time one of his lunch companions had said his name.

'My apologies,' he said, managing to add a

small grimace. 'My attention strayed for a few moments.'

'And why not, when the woman is as beautiful as the one seated in the window?' one of them said smiling.

Seated? Raffaelle turned again to focus on a table by the restaurant's window where indeed a very beautiful woman sat smiling ruefully back at him.

He had not noticed her before this moment.

He had not noticed any other women for a long time—not since Rachel came into his life.

His gaze flicked away from the smiling woman and across the street again.

He was in shock. He knew that. He knew that several important things were happening inside him even as he watched Rachel's other Italian lover fold an arm across her shoulders and guide her towards his car.

Car horns were blaring. The street was alive with impatient car drivers trapped behind Alonso's car.

'One quick coffee, then,' Rachel agreed as he swung open the door and helped her inside.

She should not be doing this. But they were drawing too much attention and getting into Alonso's car seemed the better of two evils if coffee somewhere was the only way she was going to get rid of him.

Alonso joined her in seconds, sliding into the seat beside her and sending her one of his reckless grins as he slipped the car into gear. He drove them away with a panache that completely disregarded the minor chaos he had been causing in the street.

'Like old times, eh?' he laughed at her.

And it was, just like old times, when he had used to sweep up in one fast car or another without a care while he waited for her to scramble in next to him. His handsome carelessness used to excite her then. Now it just scared her witless as she glanced quickly around them as they drove off, hoping she did not see a face she recognised in the street—or worse, a camera flashing.

'Somewhere quiet, Alonso,' she told him quickly. 'I can't afford to be seen with you.'

'Scared of what your rich new fiancé will say?'

You bet I am, Rachel thought. 'I call it respect for his feelings.'

'And a healthy respect for his bank balance too.'

Before she could challenge that last cynical remark, Alonso pulled into one of the less fashionable squares off the main street. Two minutes later they were sitting opposite each other at one of the pavement cafés that lined the square.

Rachel looked at Alonso and saw a man who worked very hard to look, dress, behave like the man he wished he could be but never would be.

And how did she know that? Because she had spent the last month with the genuine article, a man who didn't need to work hard at being exclusive and special, he just simply was. It was she who, like Alonso, had to work hard at playing the part of someone she was not.

The comparison hit her low in her stomach.

As if he could tell what she was thinking, 'You have done very well for yourself,' Alonso said.

Rachel didn't answer, giving her attention to the waiter who had come to their table. 'Espresso,' she told him. 'N-no, I don't want anything else.'

Alonso ordered the same, then casually dismissed the waiter with a flick of a hand. Had he always behaved with this much casual arrogance and she had been too besotted with him to notice?

'What *are* you doing here in Milan?' She repeated her question from earlier.

Sitting back in his seat and crossing a knee

over the other, he said, 'I moved here six months ago—to a better position, of course.'

Of course, Rachel acknowledged. Alonso had always been ambitiously upwardly mobile. 'Still selling cars?'

'Super-cars, *cara*,' he corrected dryly. 'They are not merely cars but engineering works of art. But let us talk about you,' he said turning the subject. 'You must be happy with your new lover. What woman would not be?' His mouth turned cynical as his eyes drifted over her. 'No longer the rosy-cheeked innocent up from the country, eh?'

Recalling that innocent young girl Alsono had known last year, with—if not quite straw in her hair as Raffaelle described her—then pretty close to it, made her smile.

'No,' she agreed.

Their coffees arrived then, putting a halt on the conversation while the waiter did his thing. Eventually, Alonso sat forward to catch the hand she'd used to reach for her cup.

'We had a good time, didn't we?' he said softly. 'I missed you when you left me to go home.'

'Did you?' Not so Rachel had noticed.

'Ah, *si*,' he sighed. 'I almost came after you but—life, you know, got in my way…'

Another new conquest had got in his way, he meant.

'And maybe I did you a very great favour,' he added. 'For look where you are today—betrothed to man with more connections in this city than any other that I know of. A man in possession of his own bank! I salute you, *cara*.'

Leaning towards him, Rachel let him lift her fingers to his lips. She let him try to seduce her with the rueful tease glinting in his sensual dark eyes. She even added a smile.

'You know what, Alonso,' she then said softly. 'You were a beautiful charmer last year when I met you, and you are still a beautiful charmer now.' He smiled and kissed her fingertips. 'But why don't you just tell me what it is that you want from me, because I am going to get up and leave here any minute…'

There was a moment of sharpened stillness, then he sat back in his seat and laughed. 'How did you guess?'

Living the part of a rich man's woman had taught her how useful other people believed she could be to them. 'Raffaelle does not need another new car,' she told him. 'He has too many of them already.'

'An introduction to him and his friends could bode well for me in the future, though.'

'Or ruin your career,' Rachel pointed out. 'Raffaelle knows about you and me, *caro*.'

He caught on, which Rachel had known he would do. The smile died from his features, taking with it all the charm and leaving behind only a rueful kind of petulance.

Then it changed. A sudden well-remembered gleam hit his eyes. 'I don't suppose you would enjoy a little light diversion this afternoon with your old lover—for old time's sake before we part again?'

The business side done with, he was back to playing the sexy charmer. Rachel couldn't help it, she laughed. 'No, I would not!' she refused, still bubbling with amusement at his downright audacity.

His lazy smile reappeared and he reached across the table to gently brush her smiling mouth with his thumb. 'Shame,' he murmured. 'We were so good together once, hmm, *carisima*…'

Across the square on the shady side, a camera caught them for posterity as Rachel reached up to close her hand around his so that she could remove his touch from her mouth.

'One day,' she warned him seriously, 'some beautiful creature is going to come into your life and knock down your outrageous conceit.'

'But she will not be you?'

'No.' She'd tried to do that once and had failed, had survived the experience and had now moved on—though to what, she was not certain about.

Still, it was a good feeling to realise that she was completely free of Alonso. So maybe meeting up with him had not been a bad thing to happen in her life right now.

Getting to her feet, '*Ciao*, Alonso,' she murmured softly, then simply turned and walked away from him.

He did not try to stop her. Maybe he'd read the look in her eyes and knew he had lost the power to make her feel anything for him.

Or, more likely, he simply did not care enough to want to stop her. Who knew? It was just a good feeling to know that she no longer cared.

The camera toting paparazzo had already gone, missing the moment that she'd walked away from her old love with no regrets. And, by the time she reached the main street again, Alonso had been pushed right out of her thoughts by more important things.

Buying a pregnancy testing kit took courage, she discovered. She was constantly glancing around her to check if anyone was watching her and she found herself wandering aimlessly around the shops, putting off the evil moment for as long as she could.

Which in the end turned out to be a foolish exercise because, having found the courage to buy the darn thing, she had been back at the apartment for barely two minutes when Raffaelle arrived home unexpectedly, forcing her to shove her purchase into a bedside drawer.

He was in a strange mood, cold and distant and sarcastic as hell when she tried to speak to him. She needed to tell him about her meeting with Alonso, but he just cut her off with a curt, 'Later,' then locked himself away in his study and did not come out again until it was almost time for them to leave for the restaurant where they were meeting his friends for dinner that evening.

His mood had not improved by the time he'd taken a shower and changed his business suit for a more casual version made of fine charcoal-coloured linen. Her simple black halter dress drew no comment—but then why should it when he'd seen her wearing it several times before?

But she was hurt by the sudden loss of his usual attention. Confessions about surprise meetings with old lovers just did not suit the kind of mood he surrounded them with as they left.

He did not look at her. He did not touch her. When she dared to open her mouth and ask what was wrong with him, he ignored the question by turning to say something to Dino who was driving them tonight.

What with his bad mood, the stress of knowing that the pregnancy test was still burning a hole in the bedside drawer, plus the memory of her meeting with Alonso sitting heavy on her conscience, the last person she needed to see as they walked into the restaurant foyer was his stepsister Daniella, who was standing beside a tall, dark, handsome man. The elusive Gino Rossi, Rachel assumed, by the way Daniella was tucked so intimately into his side.

Raffaelle made the introductions with brusque, cool formality that made both her and Gino Rossi's responses wary and brief. After a moment Raffaelle then turned away and centred his attention on the rest of his friends, determined to get through this damn evening before he decided what he was going to do about what he had witnessed today.

In the inside pocket of his jacket, a photograph of Rachel with her lover being cosy across a café table was trying its best to burn a hole into his chest. The fact that she had been too engrossed to notice the paparazzo who took it only fed his simmering rage. It was perhaps fortunate for him that he was close friends with the newspaper owner to whom the freelance reporter had offered to sell the photograph.

He was now assured that the picture of his betrothed being intimate with another man would not appear in the tabloids, but at a cost to his dignity as well as his wallet, plus an invitation to this evening's dinner party, along with a promised exclusive interview about his wonderful life to date.

A life that included details about the lying, cheating, two-timing blonde wearing his ring right now.

He allowed himself a glance at her, standing there looking paler than usual with an oddly fragile look to her slender stance. A frown cut a dark crease across his brow. Why fragile? Was her conscience pricking her? Did she possess one? Had she spent the afternoon comparing her old lover with her new lover?

Which of them had won the contest?

A curse rattled its way around his throat and he looked away again, wondering when the hell she had got to him so badly that he even considered that damn question?

Dio. Rachel was bad for him. She had been bad for him from the moment he'd set eyes on her. Her type, her *kind,* were poison to a guy like him and maybe it was time that he got himself the cure.

The owner of the newspaper arrived then, like the perfect answer to his thoughts. Tall, blonde, and beautiful, and dressed in rich, dark purple that moulded her long, slender curves, Francesca de Baggio was the kind of woman who answered most men's desires.

Raffaelle went to meet her. They embraced with murmured greetings to each other that showed the intimacy of lovers from eons ago. As his lips brushed her cheeks he smelled her sensuous perfume, felt the smoothness of her skin at her shoulders beneath his palms. As her red lips lingered at the corner of his mouth he waited for the expected tingle to light him up from the inside.

It did not happen.

'*Ciao, mi amore,*' she moved those red lips to whisper softly in his ear. 'The betrothed does not look happy. Have you beaten her soundly?'

Almond-shaped eyes that matched the colour of her dress gleamed up at him with a conspiratorial smile. Anger erupted inside him, fresh anger—*new* anger—leaping on a desire to jump to Rachel's defence.

'You know better than I do how a photograph can misrepresent the truth.'

The almond eyes widened and filled with amusement. How was it he had forgotten that Francesca was in the tabloid business because she loved the trouble it allowed her to cause?

'His name is Alonso Leopardi,' she informed him softly. 'He sells cars for a living and loves them as much as he loves women. He also rents an apartment above the café they were sitting at being so…cosy. Convenient, hmm?'

Raffaelle was hooked like a fish and he knew it. It was perhaps fortunate that Gino and Daniella came up to greet Francesca then, because it saved him from making a bloody fool of himself by letting Francesca see that she'd reeled him in.

Looking round for Rachel, he could see her nowhere. For a tight, thick, blood-curdling second he thought she must have walked out. For a blinding, sickening, sense-drowning moment he actually saw her in his head, making a run for it, grabbing a cab and heading for her heartbreaker in a white-faced urgent adrenalin rush of need.

A clammy sweat broke out all over him. He took a step away from the group of his friends now gathering around Francesca to welcome her into their fold.

Common sense was telling him not to be so stupid. Rachel would not just walk out on him— even if the way he had been behaving tonight was enough in itself to justify her walking out.

He saw her then, right over on the other side of the busy restaurant. She was just stepping into the ladies' room with her blonde head bowed slightly and a slender white hand pushed up against her mouth.

She'd looked pale all evening, he remembered. His mind flipped from hating her to worrying about her. How could he have forgotten the baby they could have made, which might be making its presence felt as she made a quick dash into the Ladies'?

Concern wanted to send his feet in her direction. Only common sense warned him not to make a scene here. Turning back to Francesca, he saw her watching him with an eyebrow arched curiously. Dragging on his social cloak, he forced himself to smile as he walked back to her.

Rachel was fighting the need to be sick in the toilet. The clammy sweat of nausea had flooded over her the moment she'd seen the way Raffaelle had walked into the arms of the beautiful blonde.

'Ex-lovers,' Daniella had whispered to her. 'Don't they look amazing together? He adored her once but she left him for her now ex-husband. We thought he would never get over it—maybe he didn't. He spent the afternoon with her,' she confided with relish. 'I know because Gino told me Raffaelle cancelled a meeting with him to go to her. Now she's here. An interesting development, don't you think?'

Was it? Rachel discovered that she no longer knew anything. Her head was thumping too thickly to think. A month—a month in which she had lived and slept with him, had trailed around Europe with him as his pretend future bride. But what did she really know about Raffaelle, other than he was a fantastic lover and was willing to go to any lengths to protect himself from getting a negative press?

By the time she felt able to rejoin the party,

everyone was gathered around a long wooden table. Still fighting down nausea, Rachel found herself having to take the only seat left available between Daniella and another male friend of Raffaelle's, whose name she couldn't recall right now.

Raffaelle was sitting at the other end of the table. The beautiful Francesca was next to him. She had arrived here on her own and Rachel supposed that, given the odd number of men to women, the dinner placements had become muddled.

But it was the first time that Raffaelle was not occupying the seat beside her like a statement of possession.

Had he even noticed that she was not sitting on his other side?

Not that Rachel could tell. His attention was too firmly fixed on his new dining partner. And she was not the only one to notice the change in place settings, or the difference in him. Others kept sending her brief telling glances, then looking down the table at him.

Raffaelle did not notice. He was too busy plying his beautiful companion with wine and food, while Rachel could barely bring herself to swallow a thing. And, to top this whole disaster of an evening, having her handsome fiancé sitting beside her was enough protection to give Daniella's tongue back its sharpened edge.

'How is Elise?' she began innocently enough.

'Fine,' Rachel responded. 'She's still in Chicago with her husband and son.'

'And your…half-brother? The one with the camera? Is he still enjoying playing tricks on the rich and famous?'

How Daniella had managed to discover that Mark was her half-brother Rachel just did not feel like finding out right now. 'Mark is fine,' she answered in the same level tone and tried to change the subject. 'How are your wedding plans coming along?'

'Wonderful.' Daniella smiled happily. 'I'm here in Milan for my dress-fitting. Isn't that dress you're wearing—?' She named a top designer. 'Did Raffaelle buy it for you? How much do you think you have stung him for by now?'

'My dress is not by that particular designer,' Rachel answered quietly, 'and I pay for my own clothes.'

'Well, don't bother buying anything expensive for my wedding, darling, because by the look of it you will not be coming.' Daniella flicked her eyes down the table. 'Knowing Raffaelle as well as I do, I think I can positively predict that you are on your way out and Francesca is definitely on her way back in.'

One short glance down the table was enough for Rachel to confirm why Daniella felt so very sure about that. If it wasn't enough that he had ignored her all evening, the way he was smiling that oh-so-familiar lazily sensual smile at the beautiful Francesca was the final straw for her.

'You know what, Daniella?' She turned back to her tormentor. 'Watching you marry that poor fool sitting next to you is the last thing on earth that I want to do.' The poor fool heard what she said and turned sharply to look at her. She ignored him. 'So dance on my grave, if that's what turns you on, *darling*,' she invited. 'And, while you're doing it, tell your stepbrother from me that he can have his Francesca with my absolute blessing!'

Then she stood up. The nausea instantly hit her again. She pushed her chair back and walked away. Silence had fallen around the table. How many of them had heard her exit line she did not know and she did not care.

Raffaelle tuned in too late to catch anything but the sight of Rachel's taut back retreating and the uncomfortable silence that followed. Gino was frowning angrily at Daniella. His stepsister had gone very pale. Someone else muttered a soft, '*Dio.*'

And the whole table watched as he came to his feet. Someone touched his hand. It might have been Francesca. He neither knew nor cared.

He strode after Rachel. 'Where the hell do you think you are going?' he raked out, catching hold of her wrist to bring her to a standstill between two tables.

It came out of nowhere, the rise in anger, the sudden swing round. Next thing she knew, she had slapped him full in the face.

A camera flashed.

His eyes lit up bright silver. 'That's tomorrow's trash out of the way,' he gritted, then hauled her up against him and kissed her hard.

The flashes kept on coming. The whole restaurant had fallen into complete silence to witness Raffaelle Villani fight with his future bride. By the time he set her mouth free her lips were burning and her heart was thumping and tears were hot in her eyes.

'I wish I'd never met you,' she hissed up at him, then wrenched free of him and walked away.

Outside the air was cool and she shivered. Dino stood leaning against the car in the car park but he straightened the moment he saw Raffaelle appear.

'Rachel—'

'Stay away from me.' She started walking away from both the driver and Raffaelle, her spindly heels clicking on the hard pathway's surface. Inside she was a mass of muddled feelings, nausea and the pumping, pounding need to just get right away from everything.

She managed about ten metres before the car drew up beside her, at the same time as a figure leapt out of it and a hard hand arrived around her waist.

She tried to pull free; the hand tightened. 'You know how this works,' Raffaelle said grimly. 'You decide which way we do it.'

A camera flashed. They both blinked as it happened. Raffaelle muttered something nasty as his free hand pulled open the car door. Shivering, Rachel stiffened away from him and entered the car under her own steam.

The door closed her in. He walked round the car to get in beside her. With no glass partition in here to give them privacy, they were forced to hold their tongues, so the silence pulsed like a third heartbeat between them.

Anger, hostility, a tight sizzling *hatred* that ran dangerously close to its unrequited flipside flicked at the muscles in Raffaelle's face and held Rachel's frozen in her own private hell.

If he had not drunk so much wine, keeping up with Francesca in his attempt to divert her curious attention away from Rachel, Raffaelle knew he would have kicked Dino out of the car and taken his place, just to give himself something to do and stop himself from wanting to reach out and kill her for making him feel like this.

And—yes, he freely admitted it—he had been happy to give this woman sitting beside him something useful to think about! Did she think she was the only one of them who could play this game of falseness?

Game, falseness; the two words ricocheted around his head as a brutal reminder as to what this relationship was really about.

Rachel sat beside him with her face averted, fingering the ring on her finger and only realising as she felt its duller contours that she was still wearing the daytime fake.

Looking down, she could see that she had forgotten to swap the ring for the real one. So what was that little error trying to tell her?

You can't live a lie and expect it to spin itself into the truth?

They arrived at his apartment still steeped in thick silence. The journey up in the lift was just as cold and reined in. They entered the apartment. Rachel tossed aside her purse and just kept walking. He followed her into the bedroom and shut the door.

She could feel his anger beating into her. She refused to turn and look at him. 'If you want a row, then you're going to have to save it until tomorrow,' she tossed out coldly. 'I'm not— feeling too well, so I'm going to take a shower, then I'm going to bed and I would prefer it if you found somewhere else to sleep.'

Kicking off her shoes, she headed for the bathroom.

'Pleading a headache, *cara*?'

The drawling tone made her wince. 'Yes, actually,' she answered.

'Perhaps even pining for your Italian heart-breaker—?'

What had made him bring up Alonso now of all times? Rachel stopped walking to turn and look at him. He was standing in front of the closed bedroom door, tall, lean, spectacularly arrogant, with that coldly cynical expression lashed to his handsome features that just said it all.

CHAPTER ELEVEN

AN ICY chill chased down Rachel's spine. 'You know I bumped into Alonso today,' she murmured.

The tense shape of his top lip twisted. 'Is this *bumped into* an English euphemism for recklessly planned to meet with him in broad daylight on a busy street?'

Refusing to take him up on his cold sarcasm, she replied, 'No, it means bumped into by *accident*.'

'And, having spent the afternoon in his company,' Rafaelle said coldly, 'how would you prefer to describe that to me?'

Rachel frowned. 'But I didn't spend the afternoon with him.'

Shifting out of his taut stance, he walked forward, a long-fingered hand sliding into his inner jacket pocket, then smoothly out again. He halted by the bed, placed a photograph down on it.

Rachel glanced at it briefly. So someone *had*

seen them together. She looked back at him. 'If you want to say something, Raffaelle,' she challenged. 'Then just come out and say it.'

'You drank coffee with him.'

'Yes.' She nodded.

'You then moved on to his apartment situated above the café.'

'You have photographic evidence of that too?'

He sliced the air with a hand. 'It stands to reason.'

'Does it?'

'*Si*—!' he bit out.

Suddenly all the rage he had been holding in all evening burst to the fore. He took a step towards her. Rachel took a step back. The raking flick of contempt in his eyes as she did so tensed up her trembling spine.

'You can give me a better explanation as to where you did spend the rest of the afternoon before you returned here?' he demanded.

Refusing to let his anger intimidate her, 'Can you explain where you spent *your* afternoon?' she hit back.

'*Scuzi*—?' He had the gall to look shocked!

'And then you could go on to explain how you had the rank bad taste to bring your *afternoon friend* into my company at dinner tonight!'

'Francesca is—'

'An ex-lover of yours, I know.' She said it for him. 'With darling Daniella around, I do tend to find these things out.'

His angry face hardened. 'We were discussing what you did with your afternoon, not what I did with mine.'

'Well, let's just say, for argument's sake, that we both did the same thing!' she threw back. 'As least you were saved the embarrassment of watching me fawn all over Alonso at dinner, whereas I did not warrant that much respect!'

His wide shoulders clenched inside expensive suiting. 'I did nothing with Francesca this afternoon but spend the time negotiating the price for that photograph! She owns the damn newspaper that bought it!'

'So she deals with the dreaded paparazzi?' Rachel's blue eyes lit up with bitter scorn. 'What lovely loyal people you and I surround ourselves with. Maybe we should introduce her to my brother and between them they could happily make a mockery out of both of us in two countries at the same time!'

'None of which explains what you did with your ex-lover,' he grated.

Her stomach was still churning and her heart was beating much too fast. 'I drank coffee with him, then I walked away. End of subject,' she said and turned back to the bathroom.

'It is the end of nothing.' His roughened voice raked over her as he grabbed her shoulder to spin her back round again, his face hard like granite. 'I want to know the truth!' he bit out.

Dizzy and nauseous, maybe she was not going to need to do any test, Rachel thought shakily. 'I've just given you the truth.'

'And your coffee took four hours to consume?'

Rachel made herself look up at him. 'Your negotiations for the photograph took just as long?' she challenged him right back. 'Or was your time spent on a certain *kind* of negotiation?'

He went white, stiffened and let go of her. 'You will not sink me down to your level, Rachel.'

'My *level*?' She stared at him.

'Your propensity to lie, then, without blinking an eye.'

Well, her eyes certainly blinked now and she took an unsteady step backwards. 'I have never lied to you, Raffaelle,' she breathed out unevenly. 'No—think about that,' she insisted when he parted his hard lips to speak. 'We have a relationship built on lies, yes,' she acknowledged. 'But I have never lied to *you*!'

The way his top lip curled really shook her. This, the whole thing they had going between them, suddenly showed itself up for what it really was—a relationship built on sex and disrespect, which had never stood a chance of being anything more than the tacky way it felt to her right now.

'Scoff at me all you want,' she invited. 'But while you're doing it remember that three months ago you wanted my sister. This month you decided that you might as well have me. Next month you will probably put Francesca back into your bed. The way you are going through them, Raffaelle, there won't be a woman left in Europe you will be able to look at without experiencing *déjà-vu*!'

Rachel spun away then, needing to head fast for the bathroom. But she didn't make it that far. The room began to swim and she pushed a hand up to her head, swaying like a drunk on her spindly heels.

'What—?' she heard him rasp in a mad mix of concern and anger.

'I don't—f-feel well,' she whispered, before everything started to blacken around the edges and his thick curses accompanied his strong arms which caught her as she started to sink to the ground.

Her own piece of *déjà-vu* followed, as she opened her eyes to find herself lying on the bed with him looming over her. The same look was there, the same closed expression.

A flickering clash of their eyes and she knew what he was thinking.

'It might not be,' she whispered across the hand she pressed against her lips.

He opened his mouth to say something, then closed it again—tight. Then he straightened up and she knew he was drawing himself in ready to deal with the worst.

'I will call a doctor—'

The fatalist at work again, she recognised. 'No,' she shook out and, when he paused as he was turning away from her, Rachel heaved out a sigh and slowly sat up. 'Y-you don't need to call a doctor,' she explained. 'I h-have something…' She waved a hand towards the bedside drawer.

Without saying a word, he walked over to the drawer and opened it. Long fingers withdrew the paper bag containing the only purchase she had made that afternoon.

Such a small purchase for something so important, Rachel thought bleakly as he withdrew what was inside the bag, then just stood looking down at it.

The mood was different now, still tense but thick and heavy. She looked at his profile and saw that the drawbridge had been brought down on his anger and what he was thinking.

'When did you buy this?'

'Today,' she answered. 'Th-this afternoon.'

'I thought we agreed that you would not risk making intimate purchases like this,' he said with super-controlled cool.

A strained little laugh left her throat. 'There was no one I could trust enough to get them to do it for me and I...needed to know.'

'Did you?'

The odd way he said that brought her head up. 'Of course—don't you want to know?'

He did not answer. There was something very peculiar about the way he was standing there, tense and grim.

'If you're concerned that I've given the paparazzi something else about us to feed on, then I was careful,' she assured him. 'In fact,' she said, sliding her feet to the floor, 'you wanted to know what I did with my afternoon. Well, wandering round the shops trying to fool any followers into leaving me alone before I dared to buy the test was it.'

He said nothing. Rachel wished she knew what was going on in his head. Hurt was beginning to prick at her nerve endings. Didn't he think this situation was difficult enough without him standing there resembling a block of stone? Was he scared in case they discovered she was pregnant and that sense of honour he liked to believe he possessed would require him to marry her when he didn't want to?

Standing up, she went to take the package from him. 'I'll go and find out if it's—'

His fingers closed around it. 'No,' he said gruffly.

Rachel just stared at his hard profile.

'We—need to talk first,' he added.

'Talk about what?' she said curtly. 'If I am pregnant we will deal with it like grown-ups. If I'm not pregnant, then I go home.'

'What do you mean, we deal with it like grown-ups?' At last he swung round to look at her. His face was pale and taut.

Rachel sighed. 'If I am pregnant I'm not marrying you, Raffaelle,' she informed him wearily.

'Why not—?'

Why not—? If she dared to do it without risking

setting her queasy stomach off again—Rachel would have laughed. 'Because you don't want to marry me?' she threw at him. 'Because I can take care of myself *and* a child! And because I refuse to tie myself to a man who just *loves* to believe the worst of me!' She heaved in a breath. 'Do you want more—?'

'Yes,' he gritted.

She blinked, not expecting that response.

'Okay.' She folded her arms across her shaking body and looked at him coldly. 'You don't trust me. You think I am a liar and a cheat. I give you perhaps a couple of months held in marital captivity before you start questioning if the baby could be some other man's.'

'I am not that twisted!' he defended that last accusation.

She put in a shrug. 'Trapped by a child on purpose, then.'

'We've been through that. I *don't* think that!'

'You've got your old lover already lined up ready to take my place.'

'Francesca was not lined up for anything other than to get that photograph,' he sighed out.

'Well, guess what?' Rachel said. 'I don't believe *you*.'

Now that was a twist in the proceedings, she saw, as he stared at her down the length of his arrogant nose. She made a grab at the package.

This time he let go of it.

On a shivering breath she turned and walked into the bathroom, then closed and locked the door.

By the time she came out again, she was stunned, shaken, totally hollowed out from the inside.

Raffaelle was standing by the window, his body tense inside his well-cut jacket. When he heard the door open he spun round, then went perfectly still.

'Well—?' he said harshly.

Rachel pressed her pale lips together and gave a shake of her head.

Tension sizzled. 'Is that a *no*, as in you are *not* pregnant?' he demanded.

Hands ice-cold and trembling where she clutched them together in front of her, Rachel nodded.

He moved—one of those short, sharp jerks of the body. 'You have to be pregnant,' she thought she heard him mutter beneath his breath. 'Why did you feel sick—why the fainting?' he asked hoarsely.

'W-women's stuff,' she mumbled dully. 'It—it's like that sometimes.' She added a shrug. 'The real thing should h-happen any day now…'

Silence fell, one of those horrible awkward,

don't-know-what-to-say-next kind of silences that grabbed at the air and choked it to death.

Rachel couldn't stand it. She was in shock. She wasn't really functioning properly on any level. She'd been so sure that the answer to the test would come out positive, and if she did not find herself something practical to do she knew she was going to embarrass both of them by bursting out crying with sheer disappointment!

With no control at all over her trembling legs, she walked like a drunk towards the dressing room. 'I'll pack,' she whispered.

'What the hell for—?' he raked out.

'Time to call it quits, I think.' She even added a flicker of a wobbly smile.

'No,' he ground out roughly. 'I—don't want you to go.'

White as a sheet, Rachel shook her head. 'It might as well be now than next week—next month—'

'No,' he repeated.

'But there's no reason left for me to stay now!'

His wide shoulders squared. 'Am I not a good enough reason?' he demanded harshly. 'Have our weeks together meant so little to you that you could just decide to leave me like this—?'

Stunned by the harsh husky agony in his tone,

Rachel was further shocked to see how pale he looked.

Tears burst to life. 'Raffaelle…' she murmured pleadingly. 'You know we only—'

'No,' he cut in on her yet again. 'Don't say my name like that—don't *look* at me like that.'

'But there is no baby!' She had to say it—*had to!*

'To hell with babies,' he bit out fiercely. 'We can make babies any time! This is about you and me and what *we* want. And *I* want you to stay!'

Was he saying what she thought he was saying? She just stared at him, not daring to trust what her ears were telling her. 'Francesca—'

'Forget about Francesca,' he said impatiently. 'I am blind to Francesca. I am *blind* to any woman who is not you.'

She took a wary step towards him. 'Are you saying that you want me to stay even without a baby—?'

He threw out an angry hand. 'Why do you need me to keep on saying it?' he thrust out. 'I want you to stay…because I want *you* to stay!'

'H-how long?'

'*Dio*, woman,' he breathed savagely. 'What are you trying to do to me?' His silver-green eyes gave an aggressive flash. 'For ever, okay? I want it all: the love, the ring, the marriage—the whole damn crazy package!'

'Then why are you so angry about it?' she cried out.

He squared his wide shoulders. Pale and tense, 'It would not hurt you, Rachel, to give me some small encouragement to feel happy about loving you,' he pushed out.

Then he turned his back to her and grabbed his nape with long angry fingers. Rachel hovered, wanting to go to him but still too scared to move.

Then, why are *you* scared? she asked herself. He had just said he loved her and she was standing here giving him every impression that she—

She closed the gap between them, running her arms around his waist and pressing herself in close to his rigid back. 'I'm sorry,' she whispered. 'But I've loved you so much and for so long when I *knew* I didn't have the right to feel like this!'

A sound ripped from his throat and he spun in her arms. His eyes were like twin black diamonds, still angry, possessive—real.

'No—w-wait, I need to say this—' she shivered out when she saw what was coming. 'I knew that I had no right to fall in love with you after the way I had hit on you without giving a thought to the trouble I was going to cause! Then w-we thought we had made a baby so I used it as an excuse to stay and—'

'We used it.'

'But it just wasn't fair of me to load you down with my foolish feelings when—No!' she protested. 'I've not—'

Finished…

What a waste of breath, Rachel thought as she fell into the kind of kiss that made words redundant.

By the time he lifted his head again, streaks of desire were burning into his cheekbones. 'Any reason why we cannot continue this…discussion in bed?' he said huskily.

What discussion? Rachel thought dryly as she wound her arms around his neck. 'You want to…talk?' she asked innocently.

His mouth twitched. 'No.'

'You perhaps want to say something about the way you unleashed your charms on another woman tonight?'

He tensed. 'You want me to apologise—'

'I want you to *pay*,' Rachel told him. 'At least you were saved from watching me act like that with Alonso.'

'But I did see.' He grimaced. 'I watched the handsome bastard leap out of his car and take you in his arms. I watched him kiss you as if he had every right to do it, and I saw the adoring expression on your face as you looked up at him!'

'It wasn't adoring, it was shock!' Rachel protested.

'You *let* him kiss you.'

'Italians are always kissing each other.' She dismissed that accusation.

'You let him drive you away in his flashy red car.'

'It was either that or get caught in the street by a snooping reporter.' Then she frowned. 'Where were you when this was happening?'

His sigh was rueful. 'Making a fool of myself over lunch with five important business associates, by just getting up and walking away,' he confessed. 'Then I got the call from Francesca and my day just continued downhill from there.' He ran his fingers through her hair, his eyes hooded. 'When you walked out of the restaurant I thought you were going to go to him.'

Rachel stared at him in blank disbelief. 'Since when have you been so short on ego to *think* such a thing?'

'Since I met you,' he said. 'You have a unique way of eating away at my ego.'

'That's such a lie,' she denounced. 'You've done nothing but bully me and want sex from me since we met!'

'You hit on me, but not because you wanted me. And you taunted me with other lovers.' He shrugged.

'I've had *one* lover before you,' she reminded him. 'My *one* lined up against your many who have trailed themselves past me seems a pretty pathetic comparison to me.'

He touched his tongue to the corner of her sulky mouth. 'I love you,' he murmured. 'Can we forget the others?'

Rachel sighed out a groan because he was right and harking on about old lovers had nothing to do with what they had here. 'Just take me to bed and love me, Raffaelle,' she begged.

He did not need asking twice. Their clothes fell away like rags for jumble. He pulled her against him, lips almost bruising in their intensity, his hands sliding possessively along her slender curves until he found the indentation of her waist, where he gripped and lifted her off the ground.

For a few clamouring seconds when her legs

wrapped round him she thought he was going to do it standing right there with no preliminaries. Their mouths were straining and he was on fire, pumped up and ready for her. And she was pretty well much the same.

Then he turned and toppled them on to the duvet. What followed was the kind of fierce, fevered loving that staked absolute possession and claim. He gave her all of him and she took it greedily and gave back the same.

Afterwards they lay spread across the mattress, Rachel nothing more than a slender, soft, boneless creature lying beneath him, still lost in a wonderful, sensual world.

'In all my life,' Rafaelle murmured as he gently kissed her back down to earth again, 'I have never known the power of what you can do to me.'

So, gravely serious, opening her eyes, Rachel smiled at him. 'Hit on, trapped, taken over,' she said approvingly.

His eyes began to glint. 'Now you are asking for trouble,' he warned and climbed over her to land lightly on his feet by the bed.

'I didn't mean it—!' she cried out, sitting up jerkily.

He'd moved to the dressing table; now he was back by the bed. Stretching out beside her, he took hold of her left hand.

'Oh, I forgot,' she said, staring as the fake ring was removed from her finger.

The real one glittered and flashed as he slid it on to her finger. They lay there beside each other while he held up her hand. 'Hit on, trapped and marked as mine for ever,' he said turning her own words back on her with some very satisfied-sounding additions.

Then the fake ring spun in the air as he tossed it carelessly away.

'Did I tell you I love you?' Rachel said softly.

He rose above her, eyes dark and slumberous in his golden face. 'Tell me again,' he commanded.

'Love you,' she obliged and sealed it this time with a warm clinging kiss.

'And you will be my wife?'

Warm, dark, golden, gorgeous—she placed a finger on the thoroughly kissed fullness of his lower lip, loving the very possessive sound of *my wife*.

'Tomorrow.' She nodded gravely.

'Even though you get Daniella as a stepsister-in-law?'

'You get worse from me,' Rachel said. 'You get

a fully paid-up member of the paparazzi as your brother-in-law.'

'Stung again—' he sighed '—you are going to have to work very hard to make it worth my while.'

The kiss she laid on his mouth worked very hard to make it worth his while.

'By the way,' she murmured a long time later, flickering innocent blue eyes up to look at him, 'you forgot to use any protection...'

MILLS & BOON® PUBLISH EIGHT LARGE PRINT TITLES A MONTH. THESE ARE THE EIGHT TITLES FOR MAY 2007

---❦---

THE ITALIAN'S FUTURE BRIDE
Michelle Reid

PLEASURED IN THE BILLIONAIRE'S BED
Miranda Lee

BLACKMAILED BY DIAMONDS, BOUND BY MARRIAGE
Sarah Morgan

THE GREEK BOSS'S BRIDE
Chantelle Shaw

OUTBACK MAN SEEKS WIFE
Margaret Way

THE NANNY AND THE SHEIKH
Barbara McMahon

THE BUSINESSMAN'S BRIDE
Jackie Braun

MEANT-TO-BE MOTHER
Ally Blake

MILLS & BOON®

0407

MILLS & BOON® PUBLISH EIGHT LARGE PRINT TITLES A MONTH. THESE ARE THE EIGHT TITLES FOR JUNE 2007.

TAKEN BY THE SHEIKH
Penny Jordan

THE GREEK'S VIRGIN
Trish Morey

THE FORCED BRIDE
Sara Craven

BEDDED AND WEDDED FOR REVENGE
Melanie Milburne

RANCHER AND PROTECTOR
Judy Christenberry

THE VALENTINE BRIDE
Liz Fielding

ONE SUMMER IN ITALY...
Lucy Gordon

CROWNED: AN ORDINARY GIRL
Natasha Oakley

MILLS & BOON®

NEATH PORT TALBOT LIBRARY							
AND INFORMATION SERVICES							
1	10/14	25		49		73	
2		26		50		74	
3		27		51		75	
4		28		52		76	
5	5/16	29		53		77	
6		30		54		78	
7		31		55		79	
8		32		56		80	
9		33		57		81	
10		34		58		82	
11		35		59		83	
12		36		60		84	
13		37		61		85	
14		38		62		86	
15		39		63		87	
16		40		64	3/18	88	
17		41		65		89	
18		42		66	▓	90	
19		43		67		91	
20		44		68		92	
21		45		69		COMMUNITY SERVICES	
22		46		70			
23		47		71		NPT/111	
24		48		72			